Caught Up

Caught Up

Nevada York

Writers Club Press
New York Lincoln Shanghai

Caught Up

All Rights Reserved © 2001 by Nevada York

No part of this book may be reproduced or transmitted in any form or by any means, graphic, electronic, or mechanical, including photocopying, recording, taping, or by any information storage retrieval system, without the written permission of the publisher.

Writers Club Press
an imprint of iUniverse, Inc.

For information address:
iUniverse, Inc.
2021 Pine Lake Road, Suite 100
Lincoln, NE 68512
www.iuniverse.com

This novel is a work of fiction. Names, characters, places and incidents are either the product of the author's imagination or are used fictiously. Any resemblance to actual events or locales or persons, living or dead, is entirely coincidental.

ISBN: 0-595-18737-4

Printed in the United States of America

This book is dedicated to my family, especially my daughter, Jordan.

Epigraph

When you go to the playground, be careful of the merry-go round.

Acknowledgements

First and foremost, I want to thank God. Thank You Lord for giving me my gift. Thank you to my parents, Paul and Diane Williams for raising a strong daughter. Thanks to Ms. Exum, Lucky, and Katie for your much-needed insights. And thank you to my friend, Tasha Perdue, without your help this book would still be in my head. And a special thank you to my daughter, Jordan, who has been the nourishment of my soul.

Part I

Chapter 1

Mike Anderson. A name Mahogany Fox would never forget. He had without a doubt sentenced her to die by whispering those fatal words to the teacher, "Mahogany has a condom."

Mrs. Herman politely opened her bottom desk drawer and calmly ordered, "Mahogany, put it my drawer now."

Damn, her momma was going to whip her black ass. A natural beat down the old fashioned way. She could already see the welts on her arm.

If she hadn't listened to Shanice, "Mahogany, blow it up" "Mahogany shake it between your legs" "It will be funny."

Unfortunately for Mahogany when her mother found out funny would be the last thing in her mind.

Mahogany got up from her desk and quietly placed the condom in the drawer. She hoped the whole incident would be forgotten, yet by the end of the day she understands that was not to be the case. After class let out Mrs. Herman asked her to stay behind. Mahogany looked at her teacher sitting at her desk. Mrs. Herman's dark brown hair was tied in a tight knot in the back of her head. By the way her tiny eyes were slit Mahogany could tell that she was in for it. She was surprised that Mrs. Herman did not sprint to the office to call her mother. Her reputation throughout the school was that if a student disrupted her class she would get 'em where it hurts. Being the Don Corleone of teachers, she definitely would make an example of her.

"Yes, Mrs. Herman?" said Mahogany.

"I've written a letter to your mother explaining the events of the day." When she spoke Mahogany watched her thin lips spit out each word like a robot, "I do expect you to give her this letter young lady. It contains information on a much needed parent-teacher conference." Mahogany's big brown eyes welled up with tears.

"Please, Mrs. Herman, I'm sorry. Don't make me give this to my mom."

Her pasty white chins shook as she repeated, "You will give this to your mother and I do expect a response tomorrow."

"Yes, ma'am," whispered Mahogany. "It was nice knowing you."

"What? What did you say young lady?"

"Nothing," muttered Mahogany. When she left Mrs. Herman's class, Mahogany honestly thought it was the last and final time she would see her school. Waiting down the hall was Shanice, Mahogany's best friend.

Mahogany had known Shanice Gusty since she could remember. Matter of fact, the only thing she could remember about meeting Shanice is how she bragged that her *cousin* was Janet Jackson and that one day Mahogany would be able to meet her.

That was two years ago.

"So what did she say?" asked Shanice.

"What do you mean, 'What did she say?' I have to give this letter to my mother." Shanice looked at the letter totally mortified. She knew all too well how Mahogany's mother would react. She always thought that Mrs. Fox should wear a Superman's outfit with 'W' for *Whippin'* written across her chest.

"Oh my goodness Mahogany, we definitely have to come up with a plan."

"What kind of plan? I *have* to give this letter to my mother. They're gonna have a conference or something."

"A conference about a condom?"

"Yes, Shanice. The same condom that you told me to swipe out of my mom's drawer."

"Now Mahogany, don't drag me into this it's already bad enough that you got caught. Do you want to make it worse? The last thing I need is your mom putting an APB out on me."

"Then what should I do? You do realize that my life is in danger."

"Yes, I do. So you better think of something quick."

"Damn. Mrs. Herman. She knows exactly how my mom is."

"I know and that's why she did it."

Mahogany was quiet for a moment. One of her eyebrows slowly began to rise. Shanice knew this to be a sign of hope or impending danger.

With a gleam in her eye, Mahogany stated her plan, "The way I figure it, my mom is really, really going to kill me. Especially when she finds out that I took the condom from her nightstand drawer. The only thing left for us to do is…"

"Us?" sputtered Shanice.

"Yes," stated Mahogany. "This whole condom thing was your idea, so we're in this together. Pinkie swear." Mahogany held up her pinkie while Shanice reluctantly held hers up.

"I pinkie swear," Shanice grudgingly said. With formalities out of the way Mahogany laid out the final plans as they walked home.

"The only thing left for us to do is to run away to Texas. Didn't you say you have family down there?"

They lived in Mountain Home, Idaho, a rural place where the citizens would surely notice two black girls missing. Idaho was famous for its potatoes. If it weren't for the fact that Mahogany and Shanice were military brats, they would have never heard of Mountain Home, Idaho. Now, the state of Texas was imminent in their future.

"Uh, yea" answered Shanice.

"Well, it's settled. We'll go to your house to pick up a few things, sneak out and catch a Greyhound bus to Texas."

Shanice listened to a desperate Mahogany and she did the best thing she knew how to do, she lied. "Sounds like a great idea, but how are we going to pay for it?"

"Leave that to me, I'm quite sure we can sneak onto where they keep the luggage."

"Isn't that place dark, Mahogany?"

"Probably, we will just pick up a flashlight at your house."

Mahogany put the finishing touches on her plan before they approached Shanice's house, "Ask your mom can you go outside for a second and that's when we'll make our get away, alright?"

"Alright."

Shanice's mother had other plans for her daughter. She met the girls at the door, Lorraine Gusty was a heavyset woman in a very flattering way, and she had a wry sense of humor that reminded Mahogany of Nell Carter from *Give Me a Break.*

"Shanice, hurry it up and get in here I need to wash and press your hair."

"Alright, Ma." Shanice's light brown eyes quickly darted to Mahogany.

What was she going to do? At least her mom provided an escape from Mahogany's plan. Mrs. Gusty continued, "Mahogany, you can come in for a little while, does your mom know you're over here?"

"Yes, I've already told her that I was here," replied Mahogany.

"Well, come on in then, I have a lot to do."

Mahogany sat at the kitchen table trying to figure out what to do next, but before she knew it minutes had turned into a couple of hours.

Finishing up pressing her daughter's hair, Mrs. Gusty asked, "Mahogany, isn't time that you should be going home? Your mom is probably worried."

A helpless and nervous Shanice looked at her friend. Mahogany looked at Shanice, boy with that nice hairdo Mahogany could tell that she wasn't going anywhere. That meant she was on her own, she needed a plan and quick. By now her mother knew she was missing and unless she showed up on the doorstep with one leg and two arms missing her ass was grass.

"Yea, you're right. I better get going."

Each step towards Shanice's front door was like a nail in her coffin. Once outside she looked at Shanice's house one final time.

What am I going to do?

Mahogany's face lit up as she thought frantically and then that magical gleam appeared in her eye. In slow motion, Mahogany picked up gobs of mud and rubbed it into her white sweater. The more she thought about her plan the more she rubbed in the mud.

She started a sprint towards the direction of her house. According to her plan, by the time she got to her house she needed to be out of breath. She ran about 100 yards before she stopped and added the final touch to her plan. Mahogany pulled the toboggan she was wearing halfway over her face so that the hat covered her left eye. Now she was ready to return home. She began to pick up her pace again, this time she managed to pretend she had a limp. Mahogany ran and ran until as if on cue her older sister Tasha showed up.

"Mahogany!" Tasha exclaimed, "What happened? Are you OK?"

With a straight face, Mahogany answered, "I was kidnapped. These two white men wearing corduroy pants grabbed me."

Tasha listened to her sister, horrified. She could not wait to tell her mother. Those men were good as dead.

"Thank God you got away," Tasha said. "Let's go home so momma can call the police."

"Okay," Mahogany sniffled.

As the Fox sisters entered their home, Tasha rushed past Mahogany into the kitchen where their mom was standing.

"Mama, Mahogany was kidnapped!!"

Tonya Fox turned around and looked at her eldest daughter and spotted Mahogany hovering in the doorway. To many people, Tonya

Fox looked like Angela Davis, she also carried the mentality of Sista Souljah. Mahogany always thought her mother was a lost member of the Black Panthers. But even if that was true, Mahogany felt positive that the Black Panthers would kick her mom out for not complying with their rules.

"Mahogany, come here," Mrs. Fox ordered quietly.

Mahogany managed to limp to where her mother stood. "Now, tell me what happened."

Mahogany looked into her mother's stern, unrelenting eyes and repeated her story.

"I was walking home and these two white men kidnapped me."

"What do you mean they kidnapped you?" inquired Mrs. Fox. "Two white men?"

"Yes."

"And what did these two white men look like?"

"One had blond hair and the other one had reddish brown?"

"Reddish brown?" her mom questioned.

Mahogany closed her eyes in an effort to conjure up the "kidnappers" faces. "Yes, yes, actually it was more red than brown."

"Oh, really? And why do you think that they wanted you? What makes you so special?"

"I don't know why they wanted me."

"They didn't say anything while they were kidnapping you?"

"No mama, they just picked me up and carried me to this shack, tied me up and blindfolded me."

The room was silent, Mahogany's mother simply stood there not saying a word. Mrs. Fox called her bluff, saying, "There's only one thing left to do, call the police." Mrs. Fox watched her daughter's reaction like a hawk.

Tonya Fox reached for the telephone on the wall while Mahogany innocently looked on. The phone rang before she could place the call.

"Hello," answered Mrs. Fox. "Oh, she did, did she? I'll send Tasha over to pick it up." Mahogany saw her mother's eyebrow go up. At that precise moment Mahogany wanted to make a dash for the door. Mahogany willed herself to stand before her mother like a soldier until her mission was completed. Mahogany's mother hung up the phone and laid into her, "That was Shanice's mom. It seems you left your backpack over at their house. Do you care to explain how that happened if you were kidnapped?"

"I gave my book bag to Shanice after school. I think maybe she took it home by accident."

Good answer.

"Oh, really?" Mrs. Fox squinted at Mahogany "I guess it was also by accident that her mother said that you've been over there all this time."

Beads of sweat formed on Mahogany's forehead as her heart tried to pound out of her chest. For some strange reason she *really* had to use the bathroom.

"That's not true, she's telling a story. I haven't been over there all day."

"So you're telling me that Shanice's mother is flat out lying to me?" she questioned.

"Yes," said a teary Mahogany. "All I know is that two white men wearing black corduroy pants kidnapped me and took me to a shack and tied me...and tied me up." Mahogany broke down into heart wrenching sobs. Unfortunately, that Oscar worthy performance only convinced her sister. Mrs. Fox wasn't fazed. She was just beginning her war rampage against her lying daughter. "Mahogany come upstairs with me, I want you to show me how those *white* men tied you up!" Mahogany followed her mother up the steps. She was about to die, all because of Mike Anderson.

Damn, Mike Anderson. I'm about to get murdered because of him.

"Mahogany!" shouted Mrs. Fox. "Come here, show me."

Mahogany entered her mother's room and saw her mother place the infamous whipping cord on her bed. The long white extension cord was oh-too familiar with Mahogany's backside. Just by looking at it Mahogany already felt the welts on her back. But instead of whipping her like Mahogany thought she was, Mrs. Fox used the cord to loosely bind Mahogany's hands behind her back.

She hated beating her daughter, but she needed to show Mahogany the consequences of her actions. Discipline was an important factor in a child's life, without it, they would run wild. She would teach her daughter a lesson that she would never forget.

"Is that how they tied you up?"

"Yes."

"With both of your hands behind your back?"

"Yes, mama."

"Then I want you to show me how you escaped if your hands were tied up."

Mahogany immediately began to struggle with all her might. She could not get loose. The more she struggled, the angrier her mother became.

"Mahogany, were you telling me the truth?" demanded her mother.

"Yes, mama, I told you the truth. I'm not lying to you," sobbed Mahogany.

"I see that you continue to sit here and lie to my face. Do I look stupid to you?"

More than anything in the world Mahogany knew her mom hated, no detested being lied to. From her past experience of lying to her mother, Mahogany knew that she was treading water.

"No," said Mahogany.

"Then I don't know why you continue to test my intelligence."

Mahogany watched in absolute horror as her mother pulled a spare cord from her closet. Where did that come from?

"If I have to beat the truth out of you, I will." Although Mahogany thought she was a soldier destined to accomplish "operation kidnap", after the beating she was more than ready to abandon her mission and deem it failed.

"Okay, Mama, okay. I was lying, I'm sorry."

To Mahogany it seemed the more she confessed the harder her mother hit her with the cord. It was about two minutes later before her mother stopped and screamed, "Why did you lie to me?" Although Mahogany's spirit was broken it did not deter her from lying again.

"I lied because I was scared."

"Of what?" she demanded.

"Mrs. Herman thinks that I bought a condom to school but it was a balloon and she didn't like the way I was playing with it."

Mrs. Fox could obviously tell that Mahogany still hadn't learned her lesson, but that was fine, she had a lot of investigating to do.

During her days of investigation, Mrs. Fox found out the truth behind Mahogany's "alleged kidnapping." For a moment, even Shanice's life was in extreme danger. After the full condom story was out, Mahogany's life was never the same. It seemed at least once a week Mrs. Fox had a reason to whip Mahogany. Adding insult to injury, Mrs. Fox learned that the women of the neighborhood now referred to her as "Condom Mama." Gossipers had resorted to finding out the real reason why a married woman still used a condom with her quote unquote husband.

After school let out for the summer, Mahogany was still reeling from the aftershocks of her infamous escapade. She was not allowed to go outside. She could not have company over nor watch television. Sadly, Mahogany was forced to get to know her mother and sister on a whole new intimate level. Mahogany understood it was the same level that *Mommy Dearest* knew her children. When the dishes were dirty, Mahogany had to wash them, when the floor needed to be swept, Mahogany swept it, when the beds needed to be made, Mahogany made them, when the bathroom floor needed scrubbing, Mahogany scrubbed it, and by damn when Mrs. Fox needed her feet lotioned, Mahogany lotioned them.

Nevertheless, the summer proved to be an eventful one for Mahogany. Being a late bloomer, she was satisfied to find out that her body was finally maturing. She started bursting and spreading in places she never knew she had. The defining moment that changed Mahogany's life forever was the start of her menstrual cycle. At first she didn't think it was too bad, shed a little blood here and there, no big deal. About two months later, the cramps emerged from where ever they were hiding, making Mahogany's life, as she knew it into a living hell. Included in her prayers the night before her period started was a plea to God, begging him to take her cramps away. Yet like clock work, the cramp demons showed up punishing Mahogany for all the wrong she and Eve had done. It took Mahogany days to prepare for her cycle. Finally she came up with a solution. The moment she saw blood she would take a Midol, a Motrin, drink some hot mint tea, keep her feet elevated, and pray. Her concoction kept her cramps temporarily at bay for the time being. She was grateful school was out for the summer. As fall approached, Mahogany forgave Shanice for the condom incident; she actually believed Shanice was at fault for Mrs. Gusty calling Mahogany's mom. Whatever the case, they were friends again.

Over time, Shanice and Mahogany became Siamese twins at school. The only thing that was different was their appearance. Mahogany had matured into a dark-skinned, voluptuous female. Her eyes had turned cat like in appearance, fitting her face perfectly along with her thick lips and high cheekbones. Shanice on the other hand was light-skinned and had a full figure. She liked to wear red lipstick along with her blond dyed bangs. A hairstyle she had patented herself. Matter of fact, Mahogany opted to use Shanice's hairstyle without the bang; preferring the more sleek and sophisticated look. Though many of their peers would claim they were homely looking, Shanice and Mahogany were confident in their looks. Gaining attention from boys had not made it a priority on their list. Although many of their friends talked openly about sex, Mahogany and Shanice were truly clueless on the subject.

"So, did you hear what David said about Karen?" whispered Shanice.

"No," gasped Mahogany.

"He said that she was so tight that he couldn't stick a toothpick in it."

"Why do you think he wanted to stick a toothpick in it?"

"I have no idea, all I know is that nobody is going to stick a toothpick in me." Mahogany contemplated on what Shanice had just told her and replied, "How do we get it loose, if guys like it loose?"

"I don't know, Mahogany."

Shanice did not like the way Mahogany had that gleam in her eye. Only the Lord knew what kind of plan would emerge from her head. Mahogany was still trying to figure out a way to make it loose.

"Man, I don't know what we can do. I can't even put a tampon in. She thought about it a little more before she gave up. "I have no clue on how to make it loose."

"Good," muttered Shanice. "Maybe it supposed to be tight and David just doesn't know what he is doing."

"Maybe."

"Hey, did your mom say if it was okay for you to spend tonight at my house?"

"Yea, I had to clean the whole house in order for her to say yes."

"Good, then we're all set for our girl's night out!"

That same evening they heard a loud commotion within the Gusty household.

"Get the fuck out of my house!" screamed Shanice's mother.

Over the years Lorraine Gusty gained about fifty more pounds, making her body weight somewhere near the three hundred range. Even though Shanice's father, Willie weighed two hundred pounds lighter than his wife, it did not deter him from using their apartment as a WWF wrestling ring.

"Now, Lorraine, you need to leave me alone before somebody get hurt."

"Oh, yea, that somebody is gonna be you if you don't get your shit out of here, right now."

While looking into each other eyes Mahogany and Shanice were paralyzed with fear. They held their breath waiting for the next outburst, which wasn't long in coming.

"Leave me alone, now. I pay the bills in this house not you," sticking his skinny chest out a little further he added, "If you don't like the fact that I, Willie Gusty, reside in this here house, please feel free to carry yo black ass on. Just carry it on, on, on out the door." By the time Willie tried to say the fourth "on" Mrs. Gusty had tackled him to the floor, using her body weight to pin him down. She began to pummel his head with her meaty fist.

"I want you out!" she screamed, "I want you out! I want you out! Get out!"

Mahogany and Shanice managed to peek around the corner to observe the Gusty vs. Gusty wrestling match. To their horror, Mrs. Gusty was straddled across her husband's chest, using it as her seat. Each hit she applied to his face caused her to bounce up and down. Mahogany and Shanice honestly believed they were witnessing the suffocation of Mr. Willie Gusty. When all of a sudden, like in slow motion, Mr. Gusty punched Lorraine in the nose.

Time stopped.

Not a single soul moved. Mrs. Gusty finally broke the deafening silence.

"I know this motha-fucka did not hit me in my face," she paused as if to really think about her statement. "I know you did not hit me in my face."

Mahogany whispered, "I think it's time we start hiding them."

"Hiding what?" shot back Shanice.

"Weapons. Knives, forks, hammers, screwdrivers, and skillets."

"What are you talking about?" asked Shanice.

"At my cousin's house, when my aunt and her husband get into fights, I help my cousin hide the weapons and the way I see it, we have about ten seconds before your mother flips out and tries to kill your father."

At that precise moment, Shanice was grateful for having Mahogany Fox as her friend. She was a friend who could relate to the most embarrassing aspects of her life. She felt mortified by her parents' behavior. Shanice quickly thanked God for Mahogany.

"We better hurry up," continued Mahogany, jarring Shanice from her prayers. The girls systematically collected the "weapons" before Mrs. Gusty's brain had time to register that her husband had really hit her.

Over the months, the Gusty's had a scheduled bout at least once a week. Mahogany did not comprehend their relationship. If the Gusty's were unhappy with each other annoying habits, why did they stay together? For example, if Willie didn't like the way Mrs. Gusty ate fried chicken, why didn't he leave? And if Mrs. Gusty did not like the fact that Mr. Gusty chose to wear his sunglasses 24 hours a day, why didn't she leave? The fact that the Gustys' were content with the status of their current relationship puzzled Mahogany. Until one day it hit her. They must love each other. Love. The only love she knew about was whatever she saw on *General Hospital*. She hoped that when she fell in love it would be just like Luke and Laura.

"Now that was love," as her mom used to say about the super-soap couple.

Almost 18 years old, Mahogany embarked on her senior year of high school. She had no earthly idea of what actual love was or what it even felt like. Sure, she had plenty of guy friends, but she never had someone she could personally call her boyfriend. Every once in a while she would hear classmates bragging about the flowers their boyfriend bought or passed her peers in the stores as they held hands.

She was on her way to meet Shanice at the Youth Center. It was past twilight and she was twenty minutes late. Hopefully, Shanice wouldn't be too upset. She knew Mahogany ran on C-P time. She could hear Shanice's mouth, "Why are you late?" "Do you know how long I've been waiting?" Deciding to take the short cut, Mahogany went through a high foliage area. She could see the Youth Center in the horizon.

Mahogany envisioned Shanice waiting with her arms folded when someone grabbed her from behind. She thought it was Shanice. Whoever it was, he or she was trying to force her to the ground. Mahogany refused to go down without a fight. Managing to turn around, she was horrified by what she saw. A male figure dressed all in black. Jacket, jeans, gloves, and not to mention the ski mask he was wearing. Mahogany could not see his eyes.

Her eyes darted to the Youth Center; she could sprint there in no time. The only problem was the large shadowy figure standing directly in her path. He was on her in a matter of seconds, shoving her to the ground, putting his full body weight on top of hers. Her attacker managed to pin Mahogany's arms above her head, rendering her helpless. Then he stopped to gaze down at her. For one split second she saw hatred in his eyes. a hatred that seemed deeper than him just wanting to attack her. As he dazed, Mahogany freed her hand and almost snatched his ski mask off. Growling noises emerged from his throat voicing his displeasure. He pinned her hands over her head with one hand. He used the other to grab her around the throat and began a slow, gentle squeeze. As he continued squeezing the life from her, Mahogany watched him close his eyes in ecstasy. He groaned in rhythm with each breath Mahogany tried to take.

"Please, please," she whispered.

He was in a trance when her pleads snapped him back into reality. No longer was hatred in his eyes, it was something else. From that moment on, her attacker went about his planned mission. He started grabbing Mahogany's clothes, trying to tear them off. She was a fighter, so she fought. She even took a few powerful blows until her body realized something that her spirit did not. She could not fight anymore; she did not have the strength. It was something her attacker was fully aware of.

He methodically unbuttoned her pants, shoving them past her knees. The only noise that was made was from the shallow breaths Mahogany made from deep within her chest. Her attacker slowly pulled her underwear down.

Through tear filled eyes Mahogany saw him remove his glove and place his pale white hand on top of her vagina. The manner in which he moved seemed to be as if he had all the time in the world, he seemed almost gentle as he began to open her lips with his fingers.

"Do not do this," begged Mahogany.

Her attacker seemed to interpret her plea as a wish for him to continue. Mahogany tried clenching her legs tight together, but it didn't help. He continued his exploration of her by ramming two fingers inside of her. Mahogany screamed out in agony, not only from the pain, but also from the horrid intrusion of her body.

He unzipped his pants and took out his manhood. He positioned himself above her. He slowly pushed the tip in when she heard someone call out her name.

"Mahogany?"

When Shanice had heard the scream, she went against everything she had ever learned from watching horror movies. Her motto was if she ever heard, seen, or smelled anything in dark unfamiliar territory, run. Simple as that, run now ask questions later. But the "what ifs" began entering her head. "What if someone is hurt?" "What if someone needs help?" "What if a child was lost?"

Going against the very fiber of her being, she crept in the direction of the scream. "These are the exact reasons that those stupid white girls get killed in the movies," she thought.

When she approached the scene her heart almost stopped. It was a couple having sex and it seemed that she had a front row seat. Deciding to get a closer look so she would not miss a thing, she made a shocking discovery. It was Mahogany. Shanice yelled her name.

Mahogany had never been so happy to hear Shanice's voice. She yelled, "Shanice, help! Pick something up and bash him!"

Mahogany's attacker startled, took off, upset that he had to leave behind unfinished work. A final stare from him proved he wasn't finished. Shanice rushed to a shaken Mahogany.

"What happened? Who was that guy?"

"He almost raped me," whispered Mahogany.

Shanice closely looked at Mahogany's face. Her lip was busted and her eye looked a little swollen. Shanice stared in disbelief. What had just happened? Mahogany repeated, "He almost raped me, he almost raped me." She rocked herself back and forth, Shanice wondered if she should go get help, as she pondered that thought a change came over Mahogany. Mahogany looked at her friend who she had known the majority of her life, "Swear to me that you will never tell anyone, never. Swear to me."

Looking deep in her friend's eyes, Shanice vowed, "I will never tell anyone, never, Mahogany. I won't."

"I think he knew me."

"Why do you say that?"

"I don't know, Shanice. It was something about his eyes."

"I honestly can't think of anyone who would want to hurt you."

"Well, evidently someone out there does."

Mahogany tried to rest that night but the ordeal kept replaying in her mind.

How ironic. Didn't Luke rape Laura? She guessed the saying was true, "Be careful of what you wish for."

CHAPTER 2

Time passed and school started.

Shanice showed up at Mahogany's front door looking very much the part of a high school senior. She was decked out in red-hot Capri pants, a white mock turtleneck, and big 70's shoes. She even had the sunglasses to boot. Shanice was admiring her own outfit when she noticed Mahogany's. Her fellow classmate had on dark blue jeans, white T-shirt, and a pair of black boots. That was it.

Shanice could not hold it in any longer.

"Mahogany, I know you're not wearing *that* on the very first day of school. Are you?"

Mahogany wasn't surprised by her reaction. Shanice believed the word "school" really meant, "Fashion show." No wonder she gotten a little confused when she saw what Mahogany wore.

"Yes I am," replied Mahogany.

"But why?"

"I'm not into that 'fashion thing' like you are Shanice. It's just that I feel that I look good without getting all decked out," explained Mahogany. By the look on Shanice's face she elaborated, "Listen, we can't go through life trying to please everyone. It is impossible to make everyone happy, so rather than trying, I decided to please the one person that I know I can…myself."

"Okay, if that's the way you feel. I'm not criticizing you or anything, c'mon let's go." Shanice shook her head.

By the first two weeks of school Mahogany and Shanice knew their senior year would be an adventure. They had no clue on how it happened, but everyone liked them, from the teachers right on down to the chewing tobacco cowboys. During finals week, Mahogany was stressed. The rough draft of her English term paper was due the next day. Watching her pencil flow across the paper, she reasoned that she could beat the deadline. The next day in class she waited patiently for Mr. McMurtrey to go over the paper with her. Mr. McMurtrey was her favorite teacher; he had crystal blue eyes, dimples, and a mustache. He was one of the nicest teachers around.

Unfortunately, while waiting the cramps hit. She could tell these were the cramps which required her to be head down on a toilet for at least forty-five minutes. Mahogany quickly raised her hand.

"Yes, Mahogany," called Mr. McMurtrey.

"I need to go to the restroom."

"That's fine, hurry back."

Excusing herself, she ran to the restroom. Her cramps were hitting her full force. Each came in waves of three-minute intervals. Once in the stall, Mahogany let Mother Nature take its course. She placed her head between her legs and prayed that the pain would go away. Thirty minutes later it did.

She washed her hands and returned to the classroom.

"It's nice of you to join us, Mahogany," remarked Mr. McMurtrey. Mahogany turned to explain herself when he winked at her.

"Mahogany, do you want to go over your paper?"

"Sure, let me get it."

Mahogany grabbed her paper and took a seat at his desk.

"I didn't know if you were going to come back." His piercing blue eyes probed her for more information.

"Yea, I know. I think I must have eaten something bad, I don't know."

"Oh, well, let's look at this paper." Mr. McMurtrey began to read her paper aloud, *"In the Tragedy of Othello, Shakespeare envelops many types of emotions that causes his reader to be apart of his writing. To a first time reader, his writing may seem sexual or make one jack off with his hand."*

This was not her paper. It looked like her paper, sort of sounded like her paper. But she did not write anything about sex or jacking off.

A beet red Mr. McMurtrey looked at Mahogany.

"What is this? This is a pretty strange view of Shakespeare."

"I...I didn't write this," sputtered Mahogany. He scratched his head.

"Well, if you didn't write this, who did?"

"I mean, I wrote it, but not the parts about sex."

"Interesting." He glanced at the paper, "It looks like your handwriting."

Mahogany looked at the evidence. He had a point. Unless you looked very closely, a person could not decipher any difference in the handwriting. She had been set up. As he continued to read, she quickly scanned the classroom for suspects.

"Through time the reader automatically gets an erection from Shakespeare."

Mahogany was pissed. She spotted Dawn Price looking guilty as sin. Dawn's eyes were brimming with tears from trying to contain her laughter.

It made sense, her desk was next to Mahogany's and she had enough time to complete the "finishing touches" on Mahogany's paper while she was in the restroom. A humiliated Mahogany listened to him drone on.

"The role of power has been ejaculated in many ways through the story of Othello. It was displayed by the story of the Othello. It was displayed by the actions of every character in the play. Othello displayed the role of power through love and erections. Iago displayed the role of power through the sheets."

Dawn Price was the typical white girl. She was the head cheerleader and in keeping the cheerleader tradition, Dawn took pride in her blond dyed hair. Half a can of hair spray was used each day. The outfits she wore displayed her small petite frame without an ounce of fat on it. After all, she did have an image to uphold. She was generally known for her twin assets that she proudly carried on her chest.

Her boyfriend was the captain of the football team.

Guys loved her, Mahogany hated her.

"Mahogany, this paper is um, a bit of a stretch to conceive. Maybe you should stay away from sex issues. After all this is a rough draft and you do have time to revise it. The unique approach…I don't know, I'm going you a 9 of out 10."

Mahogany was surprised. She thought for sure Dawn had screwed her out of a good grade. Maybe Mr. McMurtrey felt sorry for her because he had a sex-crazed student on his hands.

Whatever the reason for her grade, she did not appreciate being made a fool of. The bell rang, she followed Dawn down the hallway before tapping her on the shoulder.

"I guess that was supposed to be funny," began Mahogany.

"What are you talking about?" Dawn questioned. Stepping closer, Mahogany pointed her finger in Dawn's face.

"Don't act stupid, Dawn. I know that you changed my paper. Don't pull that shit again, I'm not the one." Mahogany walked off.

"You know, some people don't know how to take a joke."

Mahogany did a U-turn.

"Oh, I can take a joke, as long as it doesn't affect my grade."

"Really."

Dawn did not care whether Mahogany was upset. Changing her paper was the best joke she thought of yet. She was still congratulating herself when her boyfriend, Shane Royal came on the scene. He observed Mahogany and Dawn exchanging words with each other. What had Dawn done now?

"What's going on?" Mahogany did not say a word; she continued to stare at Dawn.

"You need to tell your little girlfriend here to grow up."

"Oh, I am grown-up, grown-up enough to take a harmless joke without whining about it."

Mahogany saw red.

"Listen, I know you think writing about erections, ejaculating, and jacking off is funny, but I prefer not to have anything to do with that!"

Dawn giggled. Students stared at Mahogany after she gave such a heart-felt declaration.

This was not her day. Feeling a little embarrassed, Mahogany walked away. School was almost out for the day and she didn't need this shit.

"Hey!" Mahogany turned around, why it was little miss cheerleader.

"I just wanted you to let you know that I'm sorry for messing up your paper."

"Why are you apologizing now?" asked Mahogany, suspicious of her motives.

"I just realized it was a pretty crummy thing to do, that's all."

Not true, Shane had threatened to tell the football team the reason why they all had diarrhea during the last game.

"Fine, I accept your apology."

"Really, I feel bad. What grade did Mr. McMurtrey give you?"

Mahogany laughed, "Actually, I got an A he gave me a 9 out of 10, go figure."

"Did you really? I got an 80%, maybe I should have change my own paper."

"Yea, maybe."

An awkward silence formed and from that silence a unique friendship was born. Mahogany got to know Shane and Dawn. Besides of being the hunk of the school, he was genuinely a nice guy. She had no idea how Dawn got so lucky. Dawn was sneaky and devious, while

Shane was quiet and honest. Not to mention his body, even Arnold Scharteneggar would have been jealous.

Dawn and Shane's relationship had been under a microscope since they were dating. Both caught the heat for dating outside their race. Neither one cared. Shane loved Dawn. Mahogany finally understood how Dawn operated. Against all the odds, she didn't give up on her love for Shane. Mahogany respected her even more for standing up for what she believed in.

Mahogany still did not have a boyfriend. She knew if she had one, her life would be a lot more complicated. She did wish she had a male companion or something. A wish that she hoped became true before the prom. She had two weeks to find a prospective mate.

Chapter 3

It was Friday night. Mahogany stayed late with Dawn to help the cheerleading team decorate the gym for the prom. Jamie, one of the cheerleaders had shot down one of Dawn's decorating ideas which caused Dawn to recruit Mahogany to be a part of her plot against Jamie.

"No. I'm not doing it," whispered Mahogany.

"C'mon, Mahogany, this is so amateur a two-year old could do it."

"I'm not doing it," repeated Mahogany.

Dawn looked intently at Mahogany and went over her plan again. "It's simple, go to Jamie's car, open the door, take the crazy glue out, put some crazy glue behind the brake pedal, especially on the bottom. That's it. Now what is so hard about that?"

"Nothing, besides the fact that it is dangerous. I'm not doing it, case closed."

Dawn asked, "Well, fine. Can you at least be a decoy while I'll go do it?"

"Well, I really don't want to be an accessory to a crime…go ahead, hurry up," she smiled. Looking over her shoulder, Dawn sauntered outside. She found Jamie's car in its usual position. She opened the door and applied the glue. After finishing the tasks, Dawn used her rank as head cheerleader to persuade everyone to agree to a quick meeting at A.J.'s. The girls pulled their cars out of the school driveway. Dawn pulled out of the parking lot feeling confident, a confidence that left when she saw Jamie's car directly behind her.

"I thought you put the glue on," questioned Mahogany.

"I did. She must not be pushing down on the brake hard enough."

Panicked, Dawn looked in the rear-view mirror. "I know if I slow down that will make her push on her brakes." Dawn pushed on her brake, Jamie pushed on her brake. Nothing happened. "Maybe the glue dried before she got to her car," reasoned Dawn.

"Yea, maybe." When it came to analyzing certain situations, Dawn had to know why certain things did not go her way. She could not stand being proven wrong, a fault that Mahogany found very annoying.

"Oh, well, it was a good idea." Dawn spoke those fateful words as she crossed the railroad tracks. Expecting to see Jamie behind her, she saw Jamie's car was stuck on the railroad tracks. To make matters worse, the approaching train had just activated the train alarm.

"Oh, oh, shit. Tell me this isn't happening." Pulling the car onto the side of the road, Dawn and Mahogany sprinted to Jamie's car. The rubber tires burning on the asphalt produced a thick cloud of smoke.

"It won't go!" Jamie yelled.

"Get out! I think your brake is jammed. Let me try to fix it," ordered Dawn.

"You think so?" Jamie paused to look down at the brake pedal.

Dawn wanted to push her dumb ass out of the way.

"Move! Let me fix it." The train slowly got closer. Dawn dove in and tried to pull the glued brake from the floor.

Damn that was some strong glue. It didn't move an inch. By the look on Dawn's face Mahogany could tell that she was worried. Deciding to help her friend, Mahogany chose to assist Dawn with "Project Oh, Shit." Getting in on the passenger side of Jamie's car, she knelt near the brake and pulled.

"C'mon Dawn, pull with me!" urged Mahogany.

With Jamie looking on, the girls tried to lift the brake pedal with all their might, but it refused to loosen.

The train was about 75 yards away. The whistle was constantly blowing. They were caught. After the train hits Jamie's car, an investigation will be done, the police will find the glue and Mahogany and Dawn will go to jail. Mahogany's mother will beat the ever-living daylights out of her. That thought alone gave Mahogany a new incentive. The train was about 20 yards away.

"One more time," ordered Mahogany.

In the same position, they pulled until they heard a pop. Dawn ordered Jamie inside the car and drove over the tracks to retrieve her car. Mahogany wanted no part of anymore of Dawn's schemes.

Jamie broke the thick silence, "Thanks guys, I guess I'll see you at A.J.'s." Like the wind, she was gone.

"Does she realize what just happened?" Dawn shook her head, what a dumb ass. Dawn bet by the time Jamie arrived at A.J.'s she would have forgotten the whole ordeal. She did. Jamie went into detail on what her prom dress looked like. Mahogany and Dawn sat back, listening to Jamie ramble on about her dark blue strapless dress.

They were relieved to be off the hook. For the first time since they left the school parking lot, Mahogany and Dawn let out a sigh of relief.

*   *   *

Prom night arrived. Mahogany and Shanice were saddened realizing that they were each other's date. Neither took the time nor put the effort into finding a date. Why bother? They went their whole life without having boyfriends. Just because they were going to their prom did not mean they needed to go with a boy. Life would surely go on. When Shanice arrived at Mahogany's house Mrs. Fox shook her head in pity.

"You look very nice Shanice." She wore a long sheer black velvet dress with a slit down the side. Shanice wanted to represent. She borrowed her mother's pearl choker with earrings that matched. For the finishing touch she had micro-braids put in. Although her head was killing her, knowing that she looked good took some of the pain away. Mrs. Fox continued, "It's a shame that you girls don't have dates for the prom. Now what's the problem?"

Shanice cringed. She hated one-on-one discussions with Mrs. Fox.

"Um, I don't know."

"Don't you guys know any boys in your school?"

"Yea, we know some boys," hedged Shanice.

"Then what's the problem? Talk to me," she commanded.

"I guess maybe we're too picky and the boys at our school are at an immature stage in their life, and you know how they say girls mature faster than boys…"

"So what you are you saying is that you feel more comfortable being around girls, females? Now, I don't want you to take this the wrong way but are you gay? You know they say people aren't familiar with their sexuality until their mid-twenties."

Shanice wished that the floor would swallow her up. She didn't even talk about sex with her own mother, only the Lord knew why Mrs. Fox picked this topic for discussion.

"Oh, that's interesting," responded Shanice. "You'll be happy to know that I'm fairly secure in my sexuality. I do prefer men."

"Well, I'm happy to hear it."

Shanice heard Mahogany coming downstairs. It's about time. The idea of spending two-more minutes with Mrs. Fox made Shanice want to cry and she hadn't cried in two years. Why was Mahogany always late?

Mahogany heard their whole conversation upstairs. She wanted to rescue Shanice but didn't feel like getting an argument with her mother. An argument would lead to hours of discussion to the possibility of a whipping. Nope, she wasn't going to do it no matter how much she loved Shanice.

"Ready to go, Shanice?"

"Yes, let's go. Good-bye, Mrs. Fox." The girls quickly left the house. "Why didn't you save me from your mother?"

"Sorry, you knew I couldn't help the discussion. I know you're not mad at me, like I can control my mother."

She did have a point.

"What do you think of my dress?" questioned Mahogany.

"You and I both look gorgeous. I love your dress." In contrast to her dark skin color Mahogany had a sparkling silver short dress that came with a long glittery shawl. Her legs looked to be a mile long. Shanice could not help but stare. She had never seen Mahogany so dressed up, so beautiful. Her make-up made her look like a totally different person. She looked radiant.

"Why thank you darling, shall we go to the ball?"

"We shall."

Hollywood glamour was the theme of the prom. The decorations were done so well that Mahogany could not tell that the room was a gym. Stars twirled on the ceiling, smoke bellowed throughout the air, and glimmering lights reflected off the walls. This was her final year with her classmates. What was in store for her future? Did she have any regrets? Wishes to fulfill? Didn't everyone? She, more than anything wanted to follow her dream of being an actress. She wanted, no needed to be the next Dorothy Dandridge and she would be, no matter what her mother or anyone else thought. Acting touched her where nothing else could. According to Webster acting was "something done merely for show." That *something* sent blood pounding through Mahogany's veins.

"Did you see Patrice's dress? Who would wear black leather to a prom? Let alone, leather with a zipper," asked Shanice.

Mahogany really was going to miss Shanice. Cal-Tech had accepted Shanice's application. The Gustys' were very proud of their daughter. So was Mahogany. They had made it. Now was the time for celebration in their life. The girls laughed, mingled, and told everyone how nice they looked. The crowning of King and Queen provided interesting conversation. Under the glimmering lights of the decorations, Dawn Price and Shane Royal were announced as King and Queen. Looking like the classic Hallmark couple, Mahogany couldn't help but feel a little jealous. The way Shane looked at Dawn, you knew they were destined to be husband and wife. First love. Isn't that the strongest love? Dawn waved to Mahogany as they placed the crown on her head.

"I'll bet she never forget this night," thought Mahogany.

She and Shanice danced the night away. Who needed dates? *"Just Grove to the Music,"* as Earth, Wind, and Fire sang. It wasn't until 4 A.M. that Mahogany and Shanice returned home. Tired and sweaty, both prayed that Mrs. Fox wasn't waiting up with a cord in hand. The girls crept upstairs, promptly falling asleep.

* * *

Graduation came and went. Mahogany's mother was extremely pleased with her daughter. She even went so far as to say such. Graduating ceremony went on like clockwork. Mahogany did feel sorry for Shanice. It seemed that her Aunt Wheatley came to the graduation and just as her sister, Lorraine, Wheatley had curves in all the right places and then some. Amusingly, she wore very little clothes to prove this. Even Mrs. Fox looked on in disgust. 'Hot Mama' Wheatley wore a pair of gold printed leopard shoes with a matching mini-skirt to show off the rolls on her thunderous thighs. Accentuating the Mt. Everest cleavage God had blessed her with: She wore a tight hot pink body suit. She could have been one of the lost Wonders of the World.

During the post-graduation ceremony, Shanice and Mahogany watched 'Hot Mama' Wheatley blatantly flirt with every male available or not. Black, White, or Asian, she did not have a preference. Just like a beast about to eat their pray, she would make it a point to stare unrelenting at their "package." Dawn saw this as her moment of opportunity to play a joke. "Mahogany, do you want to tell Shanice's aunt that Mr. McMurtrey likes her?"

"No way, Dawn, I'm through with pranks."

"C'mon one for the road."

Mahogany thought about it, she looked into Dawn's eyes that were full of excitement. She did need a laugh. Why not?

"Alright, I'm not doing anything but watching," declared Mahogany.

"That's fine."

Mahogany watched as Dawn planted the bait. As expected, Aunt Wheatley immediately made a beeline for Mr. McMurtrey. Like any unsuspecting victim, Mr. McMurtrey was a helpless one. Dawn and Mahogany almost peed their pants as they eavesdropped on their conversation.

In a husky whisper, Wheatley asked Mr. McMurtrey, "So you like what you see?" "Like what…what?" he stuttered.

"Me, baby, all of me, why you lookin' scared? I ain't gone hurt you."

Mr. McMurtrey started gasping for air. 'Hot Mama' Wheatley continued, "Do you want me to hurt you?"

"No, no, Ma'am."

"Alright then, cause I'm not into that. Oh my goodness, look at your gorgeous blue eyes. I can already see myself looking down into them as I sit on top of your face. Umm, with that tongue of yours going to work."

He turned red. "That won't be necessary," he claimed.

"You're right, that shit won't be necessary. We don't need those games, let's just do it."

"Ah…ah."

"Don't start panicking, honey. No one needs to know that you desire the finest of dark chocolates. Tell ya what, I got a maroon 1974 Pinto outside, I'm going to discreetly leave the room. Meet there in ten minutes."

"Okay, okay."

Everyone watched as "Hot Mama", the sex-queen left the room. Word had it she waited two hours in the "love" Pinto for Mr. McMurtrey to emerge. Lord, she was going to miss these people.

* * *

Graduation was over and Mahogany gained charge of her life. She understood that her mother wanted her to go to college. "Make something of yourself," she said. But what about she wanted to do with her life? Didn't that matter? Apparently not, she had dreams of her own. Dreams would not be achieved by her mother telling her how to live her life. It was final. Mahogany made up her mind to tell her mother exactly how she felt. She was going to tell her mother that she was going to California, however, not to go to college, but to pursue her own dreams as an actress.

Maybe she would mail her a postcard or something. Whenever she did tell her mother, Mahogany prayed that Jesus would be a fence around her. She wanted protection from her mother. Jesus was the only person that Mahogany knew her mother could not defeat. It all came to a head one day. Mrs. Fox watched her daily dose of Oprah and felt it was time to bond with her youngest daughter.

"Mahogany! Mahogany!"

What did her mother want? She had already cleaned the kitchen, vacuumed and dusted the living room, cleaned the bathroom, and just finished preparing dinner.

"Mahogany!"

Mahogany learned a long time ago, never ever respond with a "what?" or a "yea?" always a "huh?" and if you did not hear anything after she screamed your name, you should immediately stop what you're doing and personally see what "her majesty" wants.

"Huh?" Mahogany responded from her mother's bedroom door. Her mother was relaxed in her bed.

"Mahogany, sit down. I want to know what you have decided to major in. What are you going to do with your life?"

This was her opportunity. Her mother had graciously opened the door she was looking for, now all she had to do was walk through it.

"I want to do something that I want to do."

"So what do you think you'd want to do?" With blood rushing in her ears and lungs heavy, Mahogany said, "I want to be an actress." Without missing a beat, Mrs. Fox countered, "You know that profession is very unstable, it's hard to get your foot through the door. Actors don't last long at all! Why do you want to be an actress?"

"Because I like it." Why did her voice sound weak?

"I like eating Sugar Daddy's. Do you see me eating Sugar Daddy's twenty-four hours a day?"

"Mama, you can't compare my hopes and dreams to you eating Sugar Daddy's." There. She told her.

"So, now you want to tell me what I can and can not do. Do I have this right?"

"No, that's not what I'm saying. I'm saying that just because you do not share my opinion doesn't mean you should criticize it." Mrs. Fox voice raised a couple of octaves.

"And why not, don't you feel you need a honest opinion or are you too caught up in your "dream" to realize that?"

Tears formed in Mahogany eyes. She was going to be 18 in four months. What really made her angry was how her mother still had the power and ability to make her cry. Mahogany's voice was beyond cracking.

"No, I'm not too caught up. It's just that acting is what I want to do."

"Yea, I want to fly kites, do you see me doing it?" Mahogany was silent. "Do you?" yelled Mrs. Fox.

"No," whispered Mahogany. Tears streamed down her face.

"Now I suggest that you re-think on what you want to do with your life because being an actress is not an option."

Summoning the last bit of fight left in her body, Mahogany managed to say, "But it's what I want to do."

"Mahogany!"

And just like that it was over. Mahogany's dream vanished before her eyes. Mahogany left her mother's room, going directly into the bathroom. She put the toilet seat down, knelt on top of it, and began to cry. Deep sobs came from within. Why did she have to do what made other people happy? Didn't her needs matter at all? Apparently not. She hated living with her mother. Only "her" law mattered, no one else did. What a bitch.

"Mahogany?" her mother called.

"Yes."

"Get this telephone. I'll leave it here at the door."

"Alright."

She quickly splashed her face with cold water. She couldn't wait to move out, do things that she wanted to do. Opening the door, she bent down and picked up the telephone.

"Hello?"

"Hi, Mahogany." It was Dawn. She sounded worse than Mahogany felt.

"What's up?"

"You'll never going to believe this, but I'm pregnant."

Part II

Chapter 4

It was hot and humid. Mahogany finished up the last leg of the 400-meter race for her PE class, out of the corner of her eye, she saw one of her classmates slowly creeping up on her. She was 30 feet from the finish line. The girl turned up the heat and left Mahogany in the dust. Crossing the finishing line, Mahogany struggled to catch her breath.

"This humidity is a bitch ain't it?"

Good 'ol Shanice, making fun of her as usual. They were in Raleigh, North Carolina. Both girls attended NC State University.

"Yes, it is a bitch," Mahogany gasped as she still struggled to catch her breath.

For reasons they still did not understand, they were able to go to college together. Shanice had intended on going to Cal-Tech, yet Cal-Tech had no intentions of allowing her to come to its college, let alone its campus. She received her rejection letter the day after graduation. It was a devastating blow for the Gusty's, but their devastation changed when Mahogany inexplicably received a track and field scholarship to NC State. It was a total mystery on how Mahogany got the scholarship. Mrs. Fox believed it was a sign from God that Mahogany needed to go to college.

The Lord had spoken.

Realizing she did not have a choice, Mahogany accepted it and she even got her advisor to pull a couple of strings for Shanice. Since

Shanice's SAT scores were low, Mahogany advisors got NC State to allow her to take NC State's SAT's, which she passed with flying colors.

They were free and independent.

Without their parents' constant harassment, a totally new outlook on life emerged. Mahogany's plan consisted of trying the college thing for a couple of years and if it didn't work out, she could at least say that she tried. Shanice's plan on the other hand was to meet as many guys as she possibly could.

When Mahogany voiced her concerns about her behavior; Shanice did not care. Freedom meant, no longer on lockdown. She wished there was more time in the day to meet available men. By not receiving much attention from the guys at her high school, Shanice was like a little girl in a candy store. Maybe she could show these country boys a thing or two. Yea, she was going to *put it on* them.

She was still a virgin. It was a sad case she and Mahogany were the most sexually inept people she ever knew. Of course no one else knew their secret, they went through great pains to keep it one.

When classmates asked if they had sex, they responded, "Oh, Yea, I had this boyfriend back home..." When they asked what was their favorite position, they lied, "Oh, sixty-nine, sixty-nine, definitely." When people asked what was the longest time they ever had sex, they chimed, "Oh, about three to four hours. My ex-boyfriend had this weird ability to have multiple orgasms. He could go the whole night."

How long could they lead a double life? She was very curious about sex. Everyone she knew made sex seem like a grand event, a vital necessity to a person's life.

Maybe it wasn't all that it was hyped to be. Whatever! She was ready to begin her official sexual experience. She hoped that it was worth the wait. She wished she knew the exact date of when she would lose her virginity. It would make things a lot less complicated. It was taking far too long. Mahogany had entertained thoughts of sex. But she wanted to remain pure for her "knight in shining armor." As they left the track,

Shanice wondered how long could her friend hold out on her vowed of abstinence.

* * *

College life was different. It was up to Mahogany to figure out how to solve the problems that appeared in her life. Whatever problems crossed her path she handled them. She was passing all her classes, she was meeting new people, and things were going great. Which is why she was a little confused when her advisor, Mrs. Teague, summoned to her.

"Yes, Mrs. Teague."

Mrs. Teague stopped what she was doing and looked up at Mahogany through her dreads. "Come in, have a seat Mahogany."

Mrs. Teague office walls were decorated with posters of Martin Luther King, Nelson Mandela, Malcolm X, Angela Davis, Jesse Jackson, and Tupac Shakur. Every time Mahogany came in her office she surpassed the urge to do the Black Power sign.

"Mahogany, I have a problem. The director of IBM called to inform me that one of our co-op students has been caught stealing computer equipment and we need to produce another student for IBM or as of tomorrow, we are in violation of our contract. So, I will need you to go over to IBM right now and check in with the director." Mahogany was puzzled.

"But this is my first year of college, aren't co-ops for juniors or seniors?"

Mrs. Teague took deep breath. "Yes, they are. However, most juniors and seniors have already obligated themselves to a co-op or they have already completed one. Frankly, I don't feel comfortable having another student in IBM, not after this theft." She looked at Mahogany's schedule on her desk, "On Friday's you do not have a class. Would you be interested in going there from 9AM to 3PM?"

Mahogany thought about it. She really did enjoy sleeping in on Friday's.

Mrs. Teague added, "Of course, you would be paid."

"What would I have to do?"

"You would assist clients with information on a variety of computers, ranging from computer installation to running numerous programs. Are you interested?" Didn't this girl know a good opportunity when one presented itself? She was tired and ready to go home. Why didn't she say yes? There was an African poetry reading that she needed to get to.

"Sure, why not. I'll do it."

Mrs. Teague brown eyes locked with Mahogany's. "Thank you. Do not let me down, Ms. Thang. Go check in with director, James Russell."

"Alright."

"Do you know where it's located? You need to check in by today."

"Yea, I can find it."

Mrs. Teague knew Mahogany did not know jack about computers. Obviously she did not give a damn. As long as Mahogany did not steal anything, Mrs. Teague was happy.

What did she get herself into? The walk over to IBM took about fifteen minutes, when she walked into the lobby she was overwhelmed by the sheer elegance of the design. The white tile floor was buffed to a glossy shine; the wallpaper consisted of an elaborate pattern which she had never seen before. The ceiling held a single crystal chandelier.

Breathtaking. It even had a grand piano.

"Can I help you?" Even the receptionist looked pretty.

"Yes, I'm here to see Mr. Russell."

"Do you have an appointment?" questioned Ms. Pretty.

"No, Mrs. Teague from NC State sent me over, she told me I needed to check in with Mr. Russell for the co-op program."

"Oh, yea." She quipped, "Go right up, he's on the 8th floor, elevators are to your right."

Mahogany floated up the elevators. It's about time something went her way. She could not wait to tell Shanice, maybe she could get her a job. The elevator doors opened and in walked the most gorgeous man Mahogany ever met. His 6'4 frame made the elevator seem like a shoebox, his facial features screamed "pure Italian Stallion." He had dark curly hair with deep brown eyes to match. With the exception of his goatee, he appeared to be very clean cut. His eyes locked with Mahogany, marking her as his as his territory.

"Hello." His voice sent chills up Mahogany's back.

"Hi," whispered Mahogany.

He was fine. Beautiful, simply beautiful.

"Do you work here?" he inquired.

"No, well, yes, well not right now, maybe on Friday. I will, yes, yes, I am working here. I'm co-hopping. I mean, co-opting."

He probably thought she was the biggest idiot and the way she felt right now, she would agree.

"Oh, you're doing a co-op. Let me be the first one to welcome you aboard." He held out his right hand, "My name is Damien. It's very nice to meet you." His eyelashes were definitely longer than hers.

"I'm Mahogany, nice to meet you." She shook his hand. Could he hear her heart trying to come out of her chest? The elevators doors opened, neither made a move to leave.

"Are you on your way to see Mr. Russell?" He hadn't let go of her hand.

"Yes," breathed Mahogany.

"Then this is your floor. Mr. Russell's office is straight ahead to the left." She gently took back her hand.

"Thank you, thank you very much." She exited the elevator, feeling his eyes burn into her back. During her meet with Mr. Russell, Mahogany nodded and answered at the appropriate times.

Her mind was elsewhere, on Damien. He seemed like the type of man her mother warned her about. The way he looked at Mahogany made her want to repent to the Lord. She didn't see a ring on his finger. She bet that he had a girlfriend or something. Who knew?

"Mahogany, thanks for stopping by."

"So what time would you like for me to report in tomorrow?" A confused look passed over his round face, "I thought that we agreed on 9AM until 3PM."

"Oh, that's right. I'll see you then." Mahogany left IBM in a state of shock. She would be working for one of the largest companies in the world. This experience was going to be a good one. With a job at IBM under her belt, she could get a job anywhere.

*   *   *

What is that noise? It had awakened Mahogany from sleep. Incessant ringing. The telephone. Who would be calling her at this hour? She glanced at the clock. 3:30 A.M. She picked up the telephone, "Hello?"

"Mahogany? Mahogany, are you there?" It was Shanice.

"Yes, what's up?"

"Guess what?" She didn't give Mahogany time to respond. "I did it. I had sex, I met this guy." She was drunk as a skunk.

"Shanice, you had sex! With who?" She was wide-awake now. "With someone I met at a party."

"Do you even remember his name?" Mahogany could not believe her ears.

"Yes, damn it," slurred Shanice. "His name was Michael or was it Ricky? Why are you questioning me?"

"Fine, I won't question you." Mahogany paused, "Did it hurt?"

"Yes, I'm sure that it did hurt, but I don't remember a thing." Mahogany felt like exploding.

"Shanice, I can not believe you would go out and sex with some guy that you barely knew. What's wrong with you? What were you thinking?"

"I know, I know," she was crying. "I can't believe this happened either. I can't believe it."

"Where are you at?" asked Mahogany.

"I don't know, some hotel. Why, are you coming to get me?"

"No, you know that I don't have a car. Why don't you call a cab? Are you far from the campus?"

"No," she sniffled.

"Just catch a cab over here. I'll leave my dorm room open for you. I have to do my co-op tomorrow, so I'll only see you for a little bit."

"Alright."

"Will you be able to make it here, O.K.?"

"Yes, I will, don't worry about it. I'll see you in a few."

"Alright, Shanice. Hurry up and get here. Take care of yourself. Be careful." Mahogany hung up the telephone. Whoa. Shanice had sex. She felt like calling *Ripley's Believe It or Not*. She said a quick prayer to God and she hoped her friend got in safely.

When Mahogany got up the following morning, she noticed Shanice lying at the foot of her bed. Poor thing. It would be fine, she had a strong spirit. Mahogany took special care in getting ready for work. She had to admit that the last impression Damien had of her she looked a little busted. After getting out of the shower, Mahogany took off her headscarf and combed out her wrapped hair. Slipped on a sexy, but professional black suit. Outlined her eyes with the blackest of eyeliners, and then put on her favorite color of Iman lipstick.

Damn, she looked good. Since she had to walk to work, she put on a pair of tennis shoes. Not wanting Damien to see her in her tennis shoes. She changed her shoes a block before she got to IBM. By the time she strolled through the lobby, she looked like "da bomb."

"Ms. Fox?" It was Ms. Pretty.

"Yes?"

"Mr. Russell wants to be sure that you know to check in with Dee-Dee Phillips, the technical supervisor."

"What floor is she on?"

"Seventh," replied Ms. Pretty.

"Thank you, I appreciate it."

Seven. That was Mahogany's lucky number. Good things were bound to happen. She found Dee-Dee's office with ease. Dee-Dee laid out Mahogany's duties in a drill sergeant format, leaving no stone unturned. Her duties were as Mrs. Teague said, "Giving customers computer support over the telephone." Dee-Dee took Mahogany to her workstation, patted her on her back, and then explained that someone would train her in a little while. In front of her desk, an old man seemed to be arguing with the cleaning lady. The obvious obstacle appeared to stem from a language barrier.

"Now why'd ya gonna take these here papers off my desk?" He started digging through her portable trashcan.

"Sir, I no take your papar. You must put in trash. I no take papa from no one desk."

"Then how'd it get in here?" He questioned.

"I don't know." She pointed to him in accusation, "You put in here."

His country accent got thicker, "You're a damn liar."

They were just about to come to blows until someone interrupted them. Damien placed himself between the catfight.

"Bruce, Bruce, what seems to be the problem here?"

"This here wench," stuttered Bruce.

"Me no wench," screamed the cleaning lady.

Bruce continued, "Through my contracts in the trash, then had the nerve to deny it."

"Me no wench," reiterated the cleaning lady.

"I know, I know," said Damien. He began escorting her to the door.

"Ma'am, please excuse his behavior. He is very irrational whenever he becomes upset."

The cleaning lady still pissed about being called a wench, refused to move.

"I want to apologize on his behalf," volunteered Damien.

"Hmmm, I accept apology." She went on pushing her cart like nothing happened. Smiling, Damien walked towards Mahogany, a smile that displayed his perfectly white teeth.

"I hope you enjoyed that show, I had it prearranged just for you." She looked different in her nice black suit.

"It was rather entertaining," smiled Mahogany.

"So how are you enjoying your first day on the job?" Were those dimples on his cheeks?

"It's going great, I'm just waiting to be trained."

Damien continued to stare at Mahogany even after she finished speaking. Mahogany started sweating. She didn't know if it was from the way he stared at her or if it was just from nervousness.

He hadn't blinked.

With the finesse of a cat, he asked, "Can I call you sometime?"

Mahogany answered, "I don't think that's a good idea, you know, because we work together."

"What, co-workers aren't allowed to talk on the phone?"

Mahogany was not swayed. "I'm sure they are." She nodded to the phone at her station, "If you want to talk to me, I'm quite sure you know the telephone extension number."

He did not miss a beat. "Yes, I do know that extension number and I will call you. I'm sure you will give me your home number."

"Sorry, I'm not going to give out my home number." He sat down in the chair across from her.

"Tell me, Mahogany, what do you like to do for fun?"

"I do enjoy going to the movies," replied Mahogany.

He sat up in the chair, moving closer, so that his knees were touching hers. He rubbed his dark goatee with his hand.

"Mahogany, may I please take you to the movies. Just as friends?"

He wanted her, he wanted her badly. Whatever excuse he could use to get her to go out with him he would. The way his body reacted around her made him dizzy. He had to have her.

"I'm sorry. I just can't go out with you." He got up smiling from the chair.

"Mahogany, you *will* give me your telephone number because you want to. You'll see."

The game had begun. During the following weeks Damien heavily perused her. No matter where she was, he would make his presence known. When she went to lunch, he would take his lunch break with her. When she went to the copier, he would help her make copies. When she was working at her desk, he would call to tell her that he needed to hear her voice.

Mahogany was definitely losing the cat and mouse game. She was falling for Damien. Hard. Granted, Damien Andrews was somewhat of a pretty boy, but she liked him. Not a day passed without her wondering what he was doing, was he thinking about her? Did he want her or did he just want sex? This relationship stuff was so confusing. She hoped that she was able to stick to her guns a little while longer. Although, she did drive herself crazy wondering if he tasted as good as he looked. Butterflies were in her stomach. The telephone rang, bringing Mahogany out of her daydream.

"This is Mahogany speaking. May I have the customer's account number?"

"You already have my number…"

"Damien, what are you doing?" whispered Mahogany. The day had gotten brighter already.

"Nothing, can you meet me for lunch?"

"Yea, sure. What time?"

"Noon. Don't be late, baby."

The cafeteria was packed. She did not see an empty table anywhere. She was wondering if they should comeback in a half-hour when Damien came up from behind and grabbed her hand.

"C'mon, let's sit over here," he ordered.

He led Mahogany through a maze of people until they found an available table.

"What's up?" she asked.

He looked serious. He ran his fingers through his dark curly hair. Something was bothering him.

"Mahogany, I really, really do like you. I want us to do things together as a couple, not only as friends. When I leave work I count the hours until I will see you again." His eyes and voice were unrelenting. "You are my best friend."

"You are my friend too." Where was he going with this?

"I need you to understand that I miss you before you are gone."

"You miss me?" She doubted that very seriously, he could have any women he wanted.

"Yes, I need you in my life. As my friend and as well as my lover."

"Well…" started Mahogany.

"The lover part can wait. I'm not trying to pressure you to be with me. I'm fully aware of how you feel about dating co-workers, but aren't you willing to make an exception for what we could have?"

"No," Mahogany said quietly.

She got up from the table and headed towards the door. Where did he find the nerve to come up with that bull shit? Talking about how he needed her. He needed her for what? She was simply, Mahogany Fox, nothing extraordinary. The way he sounded, you would have thought he would die if he did not have her.

Nigga please.

She was not falling for it. Her mama did not raise a fool. Before she made it to the door, Damien had grabbed her hand and was kneeling down on one knee…in the middle of the cafeteria.

"Mahogany, please give us a chance at love. Don't be upset. Because I honestly do…" his deep voice pleading. Applause erupted before Mahogany could make him get off his knee.

"Get up," she urged. If she were not dark skinned, her face would be cherry red from embarrassment.

"Not until you say 'yes'" She hesitated for a moment. "I'll stay down here all day," he threatened.

"Yes." He stood up.

"You mean it?" he grabbed both of her hands and put them to his lips.

"Yes, let's see where we end up."

Hopefully, in love. He wanted to kiss her. He could tell that she wouldn't have minded. But this was not the place. He knew there would be time for that later. He knew Mahogany was hesitant in expressing how she felt about him. He would give her all the time she needed.

*   *   *

Through no one fault but her own, Mahogany's grades began to drop. Before she knew it, she was called to the Dean's office to explain why her GPA was so low.

"I guess I got boggled down with my classes and my co-op."

"Why are you doing a co-op?"

"I'm trying to make ends meet."

"You have a full scholarship, either drop the co-op or you'll lose your scholarship. End of story"

After she left the Dean's office, she made her decision. She would drop out of college. There was no way she would stop working with Damien. She would tell Mr. Russell that her spring schedule had fewer hours, meaning she would be able to work more hours at IBM.

That sounded like a good plan. When it was time to go back to college she would go. NC State wasn't going anywhere.

Chapter 5

Shanice was late to class. She prayed that her annoying professor hadn't locked the door yet. Crossing the brickyard foyer, a wild looking girl in need of having her braids redone stepped directly in front of her path.

"Are you Shanice?" She looked angry. Extremely angry.

"Yea, why?"

"I want to know why yo black ass can't find your own man, why do you have to fuck mine?"

"Might I ask who exactly is your man?"

"Don't play dumb bitch!" The louder Ms. Ghetto's voice got, the more people surrounded them. "You know damn well, you fucked Jason at a party."

Oh, that was his name.

"If what you are saying is true, shouldn't you take this issue up with your so-called 'man'?"

"I already did, now I'm taking it up with you."

Shanice facial expression turned deadly. In a low voice she said, "I do not have anything to discuss with you. Not now or later. Get out of my way."

"Look bitch, I'm not intimidated by you!"

"Oh, really? Then why are you here, in my face? It seems to me that if you weren't intimidated by me you wouldn't even be here. What's the matter, are you afraid of the competition?" Ms. Ghetto seemed to be taken aback by the challenge.

"Look, just stay the hell away from my man," She moved her face closer to Shanice's, making it easier for Shanice to see her acne scars. "It's hard enough to keep a man without sluts like you running around offering free sex."

She hit a nerve. Shanice shoved her backwards.

"Don't talk about anything you don't know about." Ms. Ghetto took out her stash of Vaseline and applied heavy coats on to her face.

"It's gone get ugly now."

A student tried breaking up the fight. "Ladies, ladies, please. Fighting doesn't solve anything." Shanice shook from head to toe with rage. She vaguely heard her name being screamed in the background. Turning her head she saw Mahogany making her way to the crowd.

Pushing through, Mahogany quickly grabbed Shanice's hand, retreating to an alcove around the corner.

"What happened back there?" quizzed Mahogany.

"Some chicken head claims that I slept with her boyfriend," stated Shanice. Mahogany paused for a moment.

"Was it that guy from the party?"

Noticing Shanice's silence, Mahogany let out a gasp. "It was! Shame on you, you know, Shanice, if you're going to do these things you need to be more careful."

"Mahogany, as smart as you think you are, you don't know everything," snapped Shanice.

"Oh, I don't? Didn't you sleep with him?"

"Yes," answered Shanice.

"Then what am I missing?" Shanice rolled her eyes at Mahogany in irritation as she continued to listened to her explanation of events, "I asked you if you slept with him, you say 'yes', he obviously told his girlfriend that you said 'yes', thus explaining her presence. So what am I missing?" She looked at Shanice for answers, but only saw tears rolling down Shanice's face.

"Shanice what's wrong"

"I was raped."

Shanice's shoulders sagged from the burden she had been carrying.

"You were raped?" repeated Mahogany, "Why didn't you tell me."

"Would you have believed me?"

"Yes." A doubtful look crossed over Shanice's face. "Shanice, I would have believed you if you have told me." Shanice shook her head in disagreement.

"So, you're telling me, Mahogany that if I had told you that night, you wouldn't have thought for one second, 'Shanice's drunk ass was looking for sex."

"No," whispered Mahogany. "I would not have, not for one second."

"You're lying," replied a hurt Shanice. "You're lying."

She was and they both knew it. Shanice quietly wiped the tears from her eyes.

"Why didn't you tell me?" pleaded Mahogany.

"Should I have to?"

"I'm your best friend, Shanice."

"Yea, you're my best friend, all right, why do I need to tell you? You should have already known." Mahogany was overwhelmed with guilt. So wrapped up in her own life, Mahogany forgot about Shanice. Lately, the only thing that had been on her mind was Damien.

"You're right, Shanice. I'm sorry. I should have been there for you. There's nothing else I can say except that I'm sorry." Mahogany brown eyes pleaded for forgiveness.

"Well, I guess your psychic powers left as soon as Damien entered the picture." Mahogany smiled sheepishly. Mahogany noticed the guy who had broke up the fight peeping behind the corner. She wondered how much he overheard.

"Can I help you," called out Mahogany. He seemed embarrassed to be caught. He walked over to where they were standing.

"Mahogany, right," she nodded.

"My name is Omar, I was in your PE class."

"Oh, yea, that's right." She did remember seeing him running around the track, "Thank you diffusing the fight back there."

"No problem, I was just making sure that your friend was alright."

"Yea, I'm alright. Thanks for asking."

Mahogany saw Cupid aiming his arrow at Shanice and Omar. Omar was an one inch shorter than Shanice but they would make a cute couple. He had a baby face that seemed to clash with his tough demeanor. Once he walked away, Mahogany smiled, "He likes you."

"Whatever," blushed Shanice, "What did you come here for? I thought ex-students were banned from campus."

"Very funny, I came by to ask you out to lunch."

"I don't have any money."

Mahogany put her arm around her dear friend shoulders, "Don't worry, I got your back figuratively and literally."

Mahogany never questioned Shanice as to why she chose not to have charges brought on her attacker. She assumed that Shanice preferred to deal with the assault privately which was something she could understand.

*   *   *

After finding a glitch in the computer program, she was promoted to administrative assistant. Her new duties included coordinating office meetings and keeping track of company reports. Mr. Russell interpreted her longer hours as a sign of assertiveness. She was able to see more of Damien, however only briefly. By the end of each day, they were thirsty for one another. Damien waited for Mahogany in the parking lot. Upon seeing him, she knew she wanted him; no one deserved to be this happy.

With the weather turning cooler, his light skin contrasted with his dark hair. He wore a dark burgundy turtleneck and black slacks. He leaned against the building as he smoked a cigarette. His irritating habit of smoking was the only fault Mahogany could find with him.

"Hey, Sweetie." Mahogany pecked him on the cheek.

"Hey." He looked up at the clear blue sky. "It's a beautiful day today."

"I know," agreed Mahogany. "What do you want to do tonight?"

Damien was true to his word. He showed her anyway that he could how much he truly loved her. It was as if God had heard his prayers for a woman who would complete him. Mahogany was that woman. She did not know it yet, but she was his soul mate. His soul must have remembered her in heaven that was the only way he could explain needing her so badly. He never felt this way before with any other woman. She had his heart. The fact that she was still a virgin made him feel like the luckiest man in the world. No other man has known her body or her touch. She was his for keeps.

The sexual tension between the two of them was thick. Mahogany was sure the people in the office could tell. Damien never pressured Mahogany for sex. He wanted to make sure she felt comfortable giving herself to him. Knowing that fact alone made Mahogany love him even more. Yes, she admitted to herself. She had fallen in love with Damien Andrews.

"Whatever you want to do, I don't care." He grabbed her hand, rubbing it back and forth between his thumbs.

"Let's go to your place," replied Mahogany. He flicked the ashes off his cigarette.

"Why didn't you tell me earlier today? My roommate called at lunch to tell me that he needed the place to himself tonight."

"Why?"

"I don't know," he shrugged his broad shoulders and grinned. "He said he had something planned, I didn't get all the juicy details. If I'd known that you wanted a play by play account, I would have asked."

Mahogany wanted to scream in frustration. It seemed every time Mahogany wanted to spend sometime with Damien, his cockblocking roommate always managed to put a kink in their plans. It wasn't like they could go to Mahogany's place because she did not have one. She was temporarily staying with Shanice until she had enough money saved for a security deposit. She did miss her dorm room, not that she regretted dropping out of college. She simply missed her privacy.

"Let's get a hotel room," blurted Mahogany. A look of hesitation crossed over Damien's face before Mahogany was even sure that she saw it.

"Are you positive that's what you want to do?"

"Yes." He continued to look in her eyes for any sign of doubt.

"I just want to be with you tonight, we'll, hang out, nothing has to happen. If it does, I'll be fine with it. Don't worry."

Damien could not control his reaction. Just thinking about being alone with Mahogany caused him to become rock hard.

"Alright, let's go." During the ride to the hotel, Damien tried to take Mahogany's mind off the situation. By the way she kept fidgeting he could tell that she was nervous. It was more than just nervousness, Mahogany wanted to please Damien. He had been patient and she did not want to disappoint him. Mahogany leaned over and kissed him on the neck.

"What was that for?"

"I don't know, it just felt right," she replied.

Mahogany waited in lobby while Damien picked up the keys to the hotel room. She admired the hotel scenery. Plush brown carpet, Victorian style columns, exotic plants, and even an indoor creek.

"Ready to go up?"

Once in the room, Mahogany turned the television on in an effort to alleviate the tension.

"Let's see what's on." She grabbed the remote and flipped through the stations, not staying more than two seconds on the same channel.

"Sit down," ordered Damien. "Relax." He sat her down on the bed and started to message her shoulders from behind.

"Why are you so nervous?"

"I'm not," she said.

"Nothing that you don't want to happen will happen," he reassured her. Mahogany closed her eyes and tilted her head back so his hands could have better access.

"Relax," he implored. "I will never hurt you." He was so gentle.

Damien could barely restrain himself. She looked so beautiful and loving. He had fallen deep for her. He wanted to kiss her so badly. Not just so he could taste her, but to show her how he felt about her. Not wanting to frighten her, he kissed her softly on the lips. Her full lips opened under the pressure of his mouth, giving him the opportunity to quickly dart his tongue between her lips.

Damn, she tasted sweet.

Mahogany opened her mouth wider. It was as if Damien was a starved man. Their tongues danced with each other like two whips trying to catch the essence of each other. Feeling bold, Mahogany turned around so that she was facing Damien. She wanted to be near him, pushing him back she positioned her body on top of his.

Damien's was throbbing, throbbing painfully. He could not help grinding his waist firmly against Mahogany's who felt the large imprint of Damien's manhood, hot up against her body.

It was big.

She thought that he was going to tear her in two. Whatever fears Mahogany had about Damien's size quickly fled from her mind, he was kissing, sucking, and biting her on the neck. The way her body reacted to him made her want to scream in frustration. What was he doing to her? He rolled her onto her back and began kissing her like his life depended on it. In and out his tongue went from her mouth. He was teasing her. He wanted her to want him just as badly as he wanted her.

Unaware of his teasing game, Mahogany captured his tongue and gently began to suck on it. Damien jerked as though he was struck by lightening. His hips began the same rhythmic pattern that Mahogany was using on his tongue. He needed to be inside of her, now. Just the thought of her being hot and wet drove him nearly insane. He hurriedly lifted her blouse up and pushed her bra over her breast. He pulled his tongue from Mahogany's mouth and kissed his way down her body, his hands played with her hard nipples. Damien forcefully replaced his hand with his mouth, drawing Mahogany's dark nipple into his hot mouth. Mahogany screamed out in pleasure and from a little pain. It felt like he was trying to swallow her. Her legs, arms, her whole body turned into water. Once Damien heard Mahogany making little noises in the back of her throat, he did not know how long he could keep from being inside of her. Damien struggled to remove Mahogany's pants, but before he could pull them off, he stopped. He could not pass up the temptation to see how ready she was for him. He pushed her panties aside and slid his finger inside of her. Lord have mercy. She was wet and so tight. Very tight. Tiny beads of sweat formed on his forehead. He was going to embarrass himself if he did not gain control of himself.

This never happened to him. He rolled off Mahogany and sat up, he ran his fingers through his hair. The only noise that could be heard was that of the heavy panting between the two of them. Confused, she sat up.

"What's the matter? Did I do something wrong?"

"No, no. You didn't do anything wrong. It's me. I just want everything, this night to go perfect for you," he explained.

"Then why did you stop?"

"Because I couldn't control myself." He felt foolish, he let her down. "Mahogany, it is not your fault. Listen, I'm going to take a shower, I need to cool down. In the mean time, sit back and relax. I'm sorry that I messed everything up."

He left to go into the bathroom. Mahogany could hear the shower water running. Damien treated her like love. If she needed comfort, he would comfort her. If she needed protection, he protected her. She could feel the love from within him. She had never been in love before, but Damien. There was something about him that made her want to love him. The last thing she wanted was for him to feel bad for trying to make her happy.

She turned the television off. Dimmed the lights down and removed every piece of clothing. Mahogany slowly opened the bathroom door, she saw Damien's tall frame through the shower glass.

Surprising him, she climbed into the shower. "What are you doing?" he whispered.

"I'm about to wash your body."

"And where do you want to start?" he croaked.

"Some place that needs my undivided attention," purred Mahogany.

Before she even finished her sentence Damien's hard flesh grazed her flat stomach. Mahogany looked down and smiled, "Is that a hint?"

Damien did not know what to say. He knew that Mahogany was nervous as hell and for her to come in here trying to make him feel better put him at a loss of words. No one had done anything like that for him before. Sure, he had more than his share of relationships. Relationships that were based purely on sex. Nothing else. Taking her hand, he placed it on his heart. "It's yours. No matter what, my heart belongs to you. Only you. Do you know this? I want you to know it without a shadow of a doubt."

"Yes, I do."

"I love you, I love you Mahogany Fox."

She did not know what to say, Damien did not give her a chance to respond. His arms were wrapped around her so tight she couldn't breathe. Leaving the water running, Damien picked Mahogany up and carried her into the bedroom. He laid her gently on the bed and covered her body with his. Damien started his slow relentless, passionate assault on her. He was going to take it slow. He wanted this night to be special. Now that he was back under control, he was determined to show Mahogany how much he loved her. He kissed her as if it was the first time. Mahogany's skin started to tingle, the tingle turned into a deep ache. She instinctively began to move her hips against his.

He was not rushed by Mahogany's restlessness. He continued to take his time. Kissing his way down her belly, he used his hands to stop Mahogany's hips from moving. He needed her to be still so he could taste her essence. He could already smell her sweet musk. His mouth watered in anticipation. He kissed the tiny pink bud protruding from her dark thatch of hair, Damien's tongue instantly went to work. It quickly darted in and out of her, drawing the reaction that he wanted. His whole goatee and lips were saturated from Mahogany's wetness. He softly began to suckle on her tiny bud.

"Please," whispered Mahogany.

She was writhing on the bed. Damien did not hear her; the taste of her drove him crazy.

"Please, Damien."

Giving in, Damien kissed his way back up to Mahogany's lips and positioned himself between her legs. Mahogany kissed him, Mahogany tasting herself on his lips. She felt exhilarated. Damien pushed himself inside of Mahogany. She was so hot, wet, and tight. A dangerous combination.

"Damn, baby…you feel so good," he whispered. "I don't want to hurt you."

"You won't hurt me."

"Are you sure?" He looked as though he was in pain.

"Yes, I'm sure." Damien buried his face into Mahogany's neck and pushed his body forward. He let out a deep moan; her body surrounded his flesh like a second skin. Mahogany tensed up.

"Are you hurt?" asked Damien.

"I'm fine."

She thought he had torn her insides into little pieces. She was in a lot of pain. Unaware of Mahogany's discomfort, Damien concentration changed. His hips formed a mind of their own. They slowly began thrusting then began a tempo which caused the head board to rattle against the wall. Mahogany moaned from the pain. A moan that sent goose bumps up Damien's spine. He ordered her to look into his eyes as he moved within her. Leaning down he took advantage of her mouth. Running his tongue along her teeth, down her chin, to her neck, where he deeply sucked, leaving his mark on her. Gently opening her legs a little more, he plunged and plunged until he could not get any deeper. During her spasm of pain, Mahogany could still feel Damien swelling through her discomfort.

He whispered in Mahogany's ear as he continued to pump, "It's coming, I can't hold it." With a guttural shout, he released himself within her. His body jerking in reaction.

"I'm sorry. I'm sorry that it did not last long," he apologized. Mahogany was grateful as were her other body parts.

"Come here. I love you." He gathered her against his body. Mahogany was silent. Yes, she did love Damien, but…something kept her from telling him. She snuggled deeper in his arms and went asleep with him holding her. He never wanted to let her go.

* * *

In the morning Damien dropped her off at Shanice's dorm room.

"I'll call you a little later tonight," he promised. He deeply kissed her on the mouth.

"Do you want to do something later on today?" asked Mahogany. It was Saturday. A gorgeous day which required spending very little energy, a day for lounging.

"I don't know. I'll call you today."

"That sounds nice."

She watched him drive off until she couldn't see his car anymore. Where was Shanice, she could not wait to tell her all the juicy details. Shanice of course, was still in the bed. Mahogany shook her awake.

"Shanice, wake up."

She rubbed her eyes, "What Mahogany, what?"

Mahogany nonchalantly said, "Oh nothing, Damien and I had sex last night!"

"What!! Tell me, tell me"

As Mahogany went over the juicy details, every other word out of Shanice's mouth was "Get Out!" "For Real!" "No Way!" and Mahogany's favorite, "Oh My Goodness."

"So how do you feel about him?" questioned Shanice.

"Well, I like him," hedged Mahogany. "What do you think about him?"

"Don't take this the wrong way, but I don't trust him."

"And why not?"

"Because, I haven't met him. Why doesn't he come on campus to see you or even yet, why don't you ever go to his place? Where were you guys last night?"

"We've been over this Shanice." Mahogany got off Shanice's bed and began to pace. "He has a roommate, his roommate is a pain. Every time Damien and I have something planned, his roommate comes up with an excuse as to why we can't have the apartment."

Shanice looked doubtful.

"Hello! I was there listening while he was talking to his roommate," offered Mahogany.

"And why doesn't he come on campus?"

"I don't know. I never really asked him to come or meet me at NC State."

While Mahogany pondered the validity of Shanice's questions the telephone rang. Mahogany absentmindedly picked it up, "Hello." A deep male voice responded.

"Hello? May I speak to Shanice?"

"Sure, who's calling?"

"This is Omar."

Interesting, with a smile Mahogany sang, "Shanice, Omar is on the phone." Giggling, Shanice snatched the telephone from Mahogany.

"Hey," said Shanice.

Mahogany could not hear the rest of the conversation because Shanice had turned her back away from Mahogany. After she hung up her cheeks appeared red from blushing.

"I guess I'm not the only one having fun. How long have you been seeing Omar and why didn't you tell me?"

"I was going to tell you," said Shanice. "I was just waiting for the right time."

"Sure, have you kissed him yet?"

"Yes, and that's all we've done. Omar is really sweet and nice. I've never met anyone quite like him."

"That's good. You deserve someone that treats you well. What are you going to do today?"

"You're looking at it!" Shanice got underneath the covers and laid back down.

Mahogany took a blanket from Shanice and fell asleep at the foot of the bed.

She really needed to get her own place.

*　　　　　*　　　　　*

Mahogany noticed how the world became beautiful with Damien in her life. The trees seemed greener, the sky was bluer, and the air seemed fresher. Everything just seemed lovely. If someone negatively crossed her path, no longer did an insulting look cross her face. She simply excused them and went about her way.

She did not think it was possible for someone to love someone else so much that they could control how you felt. From the moment she met Damien, her whole body seemed alive. Not to mention, everytime she thought about him, her eyes would gloss over and off to never-never land she went. The fact that she still continued to space out after three months drove Shanice crazy. Mahogany could not help it, she was in love. Deeply, truly in love.

Mahogany finally got her own place. It was a one-bedroom apartment about ten minutes from her job. During the lunch break, she and Damien sometimes went to her apartment just to hold each other. He would ask how her day been going, was everything fine? Just little things like that made her love him even more. The hardest part of being with Damien was being away from him. He refused to spend the night with her, saying that he did not want the neighbors gossiping about her. Mahogany clearly explained that she did not give a damn about what her neighbors thought.

He would not budge. He let Mahogany know that he respected her too much for that and if she did not like that he could blame his mother. After that incident, Mahogany began to wonder if she wanted an indoor or an outdoor wedding. She wanted to marry Damien.

The fall season passed, leaving a fierce winter in its place. Although North Carolina was famous for being hot and humid during the summer months, the winter season wasn't picnic. Mahogany was in bed sick with a fever. She was thankful that she had enough sense to call off sick. She was hot one minute and freezing the next. The phone rang, Mahogany refused to pick it up. She listened as the answering machine screened the call.

"Baby, pick up the phone."

She reached for the cordless on the nightstand.

"Yes, Damien."

"How are you doing? Do you need anything? I'm going to come over for lunch."

"No, thanks. I'm fine. I've taken some Nyquil so I should be drifting off soon."

She sounded horrible.

"Good, good. I'm going to come over though."

"Alright, see you when you get here."

Mahogany hung up the telephone. Not soon after Damien awoke her, patting her forehead with a cool cloth.

"Hey, stranger," he whispered.

"Hey." She felt so hot. She knew that she looked miserable.

"I'm going to get you some water." When he returned, Mahogany sat up in the bed. Her nightgown did a horrible job of covering her up. Embarrassingly, he felt himself becoming aroused.

"Thank you." The cool refreshment was a welcome relief to her scratchy throat. She noticed Damien strangely staring at her.

"Why are you looking at me like that?"

He pushed a piece of hair out of her face, "I'm just thinking about what the doctors say about curing a fever."

"And what do they say?" Mahogany became as intrigued. He began kissing her ear.

"They say it's best if you sweat out your fever." Mahogany heart throbbed. The more she and Damien had sex, made love, fucked, the more she learned about her femininity. It was interesting how her body craved sex. Damien climbed on top of her, quickly getting rid of her flimsy nightgown.

"Open you legs," he ordered. Mahogany obliged him, within seconds his rock hard flesh was deeply imbedded inside of her. Using his hands, Damien grabbed underneath Mahogany's buttocks. As far as he was concerned he was not deep enough inside of her. He positioned her to where he could have maximum penetration. Once he had it, he began to thrust violently. He closed his eyes in concentration. He did not want the sensation to overtake him. He heard Mahogany whispering his name.

He was about to lose it. He quickly flipped around so that Mahogany was a top him.

"What are you doing?" she panted.

"Ride it." Damien took a deep breath, "Please, baby, ride it."

"Show me how."

"Just go up and down on it." Always one to listen, Mahogany awkwardly moved up and down.

"Mahogany," moaned Damien.

It was the first time that Damien had said her name during sex. By him saying her name gave Mahogany a strange sense of power. She used the balls of her feet to control the rhythm of her going up and down on Damien. The faster she went the louder he moaned her name.

"Maho…Mahogan…I'm losing it." She drained the life out of him.

Mahogany pumping, she let out a scream just as Damien captured her lips in a passionate kiss. She collapsed on his chest. The sheets were soaked from their lovemaking and the air smelled of sex.

"I love you," he caressed the small of her back.

"I love you, too." Responded Mahogany.

Damien's chest got tight with emotion, "Do you realize that was the first time you said that you loved me?" She looked into his eyes, "I've always loved you." Damien glanced at his watch.

"Oh, shit. I'm late."

Mahogany watched in amusement as he ran into the bathroom for a quick shower. He hurriedly put on his clothes and with a quick, "I love you." He was out the door.

*   *   *

It was a very busy day at work. Not to mention the days Mahogany was out sick did not help. Work orders were piled high on her desk.

Everyone ran around trying to do one thing or another. She hadn't seen Damien all day. He called early in the morning saying he could not pick her up this morning, something about doing his roommate a favor.

His roommate really pissed her off. Lately, Damien showed a lack of interest in her. His roommate seemed to be his number one priority. Somewhere down the line Mahogany had been down graded to nothing. Which was fine. Mahogany could not stand him whispering sweet nothings in her ear and then turn around and treat her like shit.

She missed him already.

"Mahogany!" yelled Mr. Russell.

"Take these contracts to the Laser Corp. meeting up stairs and tell Damien that I forgot that I had a telephone conference, so I should be there shortly."

Good. She needed a break from this jungle. On the elevator, she couldn't help contain her excitement. She needed to see him.

The meeting for Laser Corporation hadn't started so she didn't see Damien. The room was filled with business suits trying to look important. Mahogany was about to leave when she overheard a conversation.

"Have you seen what they're asking for? You could think we would get fringe benefits because of Yvette," the lady directed everyone's attention to a beautiful looking black woman as she continued, "Yvette can't you get Damien to give us a discount? I mean you guys are practically married."

The blood rushed out of her face. There had to be another Damien.

"Very funny," laughed Yvette. "I'll try to renegotiate after I've officially became Mrs. Damien Andrews."

Mahogany stood there frozen. Staring at this beautiful lady who intimately knew Damien. She knew what it felt like to be kissed by him, to be held by him, and knew in detail how he made love. She could barely control the hatred she felt for this lady she hardly knew. The boardroom became a blurry vision.

"Speaking of the devil."

Mahogany watched as Yvette got up to greet Damien

"Hey, Boo." She kissed him softly on the lips. Damien didn't notice Mahogany in the side doorway. He became aware of her presence just in time to see a tear roll down her cheek. His life would never be the same again. During the months that he and Mahogany were involved, he couldn't stand lying to her. He did not know why he hurt her; maybe in the beginning it was the thrill of the chase. Yet, before he knew it Mahogany had captured his heart. Looking into her brown eyes, he wanted to tell her how sorry he was and that he loved her. But how can he find the nerve? There was no reasonable explanation that he could offer. Mahogany watched as Yvette placed her arms around Damien's waist.

She needed to leave before she caused a scene or broke down. Which ever came first. She slammed the contracts into Damien's chest as she left the conference room.

"What was that about?" inquired Yvette.

"I have no idea," he lied.

"I bet something else has an idea," sneered Yvette. She could not believe this motha-fucka had the audacity sleep with one of his co-workers. She was used to Damien's flirtatious behavior with other women. Other women he swore that he wasn't sleeping with. Maybe that little tart who left the room in tears realized that she was just like the "other" women. Yvette could not wait to be alone with Damien. She wanted to make him pay for embarrassing her.

"Don't start Yvette, let's get this meeting started." Listening from the hallway, Mahogany realized that he was a bitch. And she hated him.

Chapter 6

Who knew love could hurt so badly? Mahogany stayed holed up in her apartment for a week after seeing Damien with Yvette. She explained to Mr. Russell that she was deathly ill. She hadn't been back to work since.

How could anyone lie to someone if they loved them? He did not love her. She realized that she was just a piece of ass to him. Did he get a thrill by sleeping with two women at the same time? She hated him. He had the nerve to leave "I love you" messages on her machine. He came over to her apartment the first three days. Mahogany dead bolted the door and listened to him plead from the outside. Like a fool she was tempted to open the door, but instead she closed her eyes and imagined him with Yvette. Her chest was still aching from the pain in her heart. She loved him. She loved him so much that it hurt.

She never wanted to see him again.

She was going to quit IBM. No. What was she going to do? She could not face Damien. She would not. He probably laughed every single time they made love. What a fool. What was the name of that song? "*It takes a fool to learn that love don't love nobody.*"

Yes, she was a fool alright. Mahogany made a vain attempt to hold back her tears, but they flowed just as freely as they did a week ago. She had to stop crying, she was stronger than this. She would be damned if she let a bitch like Damien get the best of her. She cried herself to sleep.

Her stomach growled, awaking her from sleep. When was the last time she ate? At least her appetite was returning. She went into the bathroom to wash her face. Her eyes were red and puffy. Looking into the mirror she realized cold water was not going to help. She looked miserable. Hopefully, no one would recognize her. She put a ball cap over her head and left to get something to eat.

Damien sat outside of her door.

"I'm sorry, Mahogany, please…please listen to me." He looked just as miserable as Mahogany did if not worse. She closed the door behind her.

"Damien, please leave. I don't want to see you." She brushed past him.

"Please, listen." Fighting against common sense, Mahogany looked down into the deep pools of his brown eyes. His eyes were brimming with tears. She missed him.

She re-opened the door to her apartment. The lights were turned off. The only way they were able to see was because of the stove light Mahogany always left on. The darkness was her comfort.

"Come in."

Damien got up, his tall frame overpowering Mahogany. He followed her inside. Their eyes were hungry for each other.

"What, Damien? What do you want?" Mahogany's sharp tone unbelievably conveyed that she controlled the discussion.

"I need to tell you the truth," he responded.

"Don't you think it's a little late for that? I mean, you're engaged to be married."

"Let me explain. We're not engaged, she says we are, but I never asked her to marry me."

"You think that really makes a difference? You have been sleeping with her. Making love to her!" She turned her back. She couldn't do this, not now. She was about to start crying, she refused to let him see how much he hurt her.

"Mahogany, you are right. I'm not going to lie to you."

"How long have you guys been together?" She needed to know. She didn't know why but she did. How long had he been lying to her? Making a fool out of her? If she knew, maybe it would kill some of the love that she still had for him.

"Three years." Damien did not know what else to say to Mahogany.

"Damien, I need you to leave." Three years! He was not going to leave his fiancé if he had not done it by now, he wasn't going to. For what? Her? No, he had no intentions of breaking up his comfortable happy home.

"I never wanted to hurt you." He saw the pain in her eyes.

"Well, you did. It's done, you can't fix it. Just leave me alone. Please, leave." He tried grabbing her hand, but she quickly jerked it away. He wiped a tear from his eye.

"I don't love her, I love you." She shook her head in denial.

"I love you, baby, I do." He grabbed her head between his hands, "stop saying I don't love you, I do, honest to God I do." He wrapped his hands around her body, hugging her, trying to mold her body into his. For one second Mahogany let her body relax into Damien's. Her soul missed him.

"I love you, Mahogany. I love you." He said it over and over again until she really did believe him. He did love her, albeit selfishly. He did not want to lose anyone. He loved Mahogany. She was the only person that made him feel that he could do anything. He needed someone like her in his life. It was what he had been missing. She was his for keeps. She gave herself to him and her refused to let he go.

Mahogany allowed Damien's lips to taste her. His lips were unrelentless in his quest for Mahogany acquiesce. She fought him.

"Please, let me taste you." Mahogany had a battle raging within herself. Her brain screamed, "No," while the rest of her body moved with Damien's. Just one last time reasoned Mahogany. One last time to be with him. She traced the outline of Damien's lips with her tongue, reveling in the reaction she drew from him. Damien's knees went weak. He had intentions on carrying Mahogany into the bedroom, but he needed her now. He gently lowered her onto the floor. He was determined to express his love to her. Removing her clothes, he found what he was looking for. His mouth was hot on Mahogany womaness.

"You taste good."

She deserved this. After putting up with all his bullshit, she deserved to have him make her body scream. Damien heard Mahogany moaning, her back was already arched off the floor.

"Put it in," begged Mahogany. "Put in it."

He pretended not to hear her. He forcefully held her hips down while his tongue had its way with her. She grabbed a fistful of his curly hair.

"Put it in now." He looked into her eyes, they were drunk with arousal. Dragging himself away from his project, he plunged himself into her tight honey. With each thrust, he managed to break through Mahogany's strong will of resistance.

"Do you love me, Mahogany?" She refused to answer. He slowly stopped the tempo of his thrust. It nearly killed him, but he quit moving within her.

"Do you love me, Mahogany?" He needed to know. With her throbbing, her heart beating, she told him the truth.

"I love you, Damien."

Like a musical conductor controlling an orchestra, Damien made Mahogany body explode several times during the night. And he was nowhere near being finish. She was going to understand that he loved her, no one else but her.

     *   *   *

"Why are you still seeing him? Mahogany, let's be real. Damien is having his cake and eating it too. I know that you love him, but he's hurting you."

Mahogany heard Shanice talking, but she was not listening to her. Shanice did not understand the situation she was in. They were seated in a trendy Italian restaurant waiting for their food. Shanice watched as Mahogany sipped her water.

How could her friend be so stupid? When Mahogany told her what happened with "big" swinging Damien and his chicken head, Shanice was furious. She knew there was a reason she did not trust him. Anytime a man allowed his "roommate" to get in the way of him having sex, there definitely was a problem. Poor Mahogany, she was too caught up with Damien to see through his lies.

"Shanice, I know you think that I'm crazy for trusting him, but the truth of the matter is I want to believe him." She paused for a moment, "When he tells me that he's leaving her, I want that to happen. I believe in him."

"Then why hadn't he?" pounced Shanice.

"He's trying to. He has a lot of money tied-up with her. He doesn't want her lashing out and taking all of it."

Lies, lies, lies. She could talk to Mahogany until the cows came home. Mahogany obviously had her mind made up when it came to Damien Andrews.

"What are you going to order?"

Staring at the menu, Mahogany murmured, "I don't know." He mind was elsewhere. What Damien was doing?

* * *

Mahogany tried keeping it together. She arrived late to work, she didn't have the notes prepared for the upcoming meeting, and Mr. Russell was headed in her direction.

"Mahogany, are the Jones Data reports ready?"

"No, not yet. I'll have them ready in thirty minutes."

"That's great, but I needed them ten minutes ago."

"I know, Mr. Russell. I've just been busy with other projects and I got boggled down with other things."

Mr. Russell exhaled a deep breath. His bushy eyebrows gathered in concern.

"Mahogany, is there anything going on that I should know about?" He liked her, she was a good kid, but he had to admit that she had been falling short of her usual performance.

"No, not that I could think of."

"I care about you. You've got a good head on your shoulders. But I can't keep tolerating slack behavior when it comes to work. This company has an image to uphold and I can't keep you here if you're not a part of that image."

"I understand, Mr. Russell."

"Good, now shape up because I don't want to fire you."

Great, she's about to get fired. She was tired. Damien called at 3AM explaining why he hadn't seen her in the past week. Nothing but excuses and more excuses. Adding insult to injury, Shanice kept calling her, inviting her to parties and get togethers.

Why couldn't everyone just leave her alone? Like she really wanted to go somewhere and watch Shanice and Omar hugged up on one another. Whatever with that love shit. She did not need it. It was already one o'clock and Damien had not bothered to call or come by. She assumed it was over. As she went to punch out, she hoped that he would be waiting for her at the time clock. She swiped her card, expecting Damien to be there. He wasn't. Holding her head up high, Mahogany went home. She managed to make it to the privacy of her apartment before she broke down sobbing. As she cried herself to sleep, she vowed that he would never have the power to hurt her again. Never.

He would no longer have a hold on her heart.

* * *

Damien's world continued to crumble around him.

"What the fuck are you still doing here?" yelled Yvette. Veins were bulging in her neck.

"Yvette, don't do this," pleaded Damien.

"Didn't I just tell you to get the fuck out?" She poked her finger into Damien's chest, "Why don't you take your begging ass to your little playmate at work?"

Damien did not say a word. He continued to watch as Yvette piled his belongings by the door.

"I told you it was over, I've stopped seeing her." It was true. He hadn't seen Mahogany in over a week. When he decided to call her he didn't plan on Yvette eavesdropping on his conversation. Yvette had heard an earful of "I love you's" and "I can't wait to be with you." He was busted, red handed.

"Is that why I just heard you tell her that you love her? Damn it, Damien! Don't play with my fuckin' intelligence. Just take your shit and leave," she demanded.

"Yvette, please, you know I love you. We've been together for almost for four years, please don't throw it all away for one mistake I foolishly made."

Yvette had had enough of Damien. Every time she turned her back Damien had claimed that he "accidentally" had fallen into some woman. Oh, and by the way can she please forgive him? No! Not here, not today, not tomorrow. Her spirit was tired. Damien needed to grow up and realize his God given mission was not to see how many women he could possibly have sex with.

"No, you gotta go. If you don't, I'm positive we'll be replaying this same scene three months from now."

"I love…"

"You don't love anyone but yourself. Matter of fact do you even know what *real* love is?"

Aware that he was losing the battle, he said anything he could think of.

"Maybe, I don't know what love is, but I love you." It was weird but true. He had known Yvette since college. They were always together. She had been there during the roughest parts of his life and he wasn't ready to let her go. Not yet. He knew Mahogany would be devastated, but he also knew that she would always be there for him.

"And I'm sure you love your playmate at work right?"

"Not like I love you," he offered.

"Damien, don't you see something wrong with that picture? Do you think it's all right for you to be in love with two women at the same time? If you do there is something deeply wrong with you and I'm not about to waste my life while you figure it out. Good-Bye!"

Yvette graciously held the door open so Damien could leave. Defeated, he picked up his belongings and left. While leaning against the door Yvette hoped she never saw him again. She felt a heavy weight lift off her shoulders.

Chapter 7

Mahogany rose out of bed to prepare breakfast. She was in the mood for scrambled eggs, hash brown, and some oven cooked bacon. Betty Crocker watch out! She turned on the CD player and put in Marvin Gaye, "Let's Get It On" pumped out over the speakers. Yea, sing it, Marvin, sing it. She was cracking the eggs to the rhythm of the music when two big arms picked her up and embraced her in a bear hug.

"Damien, let me go! Don't you see me trying to cook?"

"Say 'Uncle', say 'Uncle'" he ordered.

"Uncle!" shouted Mahogany. He put her down and smacked her on the behind.

"Woman! What are you fixing me for breakfast?"

"Some bacon, eggs, and hash browns," replied Mahogany.

"Good, I would hate to punish you for being bad," he threatened. He tried giving Mahogany a kiss, but she backed away from him.

"Someone has morning breath that's doing some serious Bruce Lee kickin'."

"Oh, you got jokes." Mahogany shrugged her shoulders and went back to cooking. He quickly grabbed her, kissing her squarely on the mouth.

"Ouch, my mouth is burning!" screamed Mahogany.

"Very funny," he laughed. "When I come out of the shower my meal better be ready."

Mahogany shook her head in amusement, who would have thought they would have lasted this long. A year had passed since Damien showed up at her doorstep explaining how he left his ex. Mahogany was overjoyed that Damien had chosen to be with her and no one else. She never asked him what went down between him and his ex. She could tell that whatever happened had been painful, his eyes were bloodshot when arrived at her apartment. She did not care about the who's and the why's, just as long as he was with her. Shanice did not seem too enthused with Damien. However, she was too wrapped up in Omar to concern herself with Mahogany's drama. Shanice and Omar had been hot and heavy for the last couple of years. While Omar appeared to be one of the hardest thugs Mahogany had met, Shanice bought out a gentleness inside of him that made Mahogany a little jealous. Not that she was complaining about Damien, but one could look into Omar eyes and unequivocally see that he deeply loved and cared about Shanice. It was like, she was his whole world.

Damien came out of the shower wearing only a towel around his waist.

"Do you want me to fix you a plate," asked Mahogany.

"Yea, baby. Thanks." Mahogany piled his plate high with food.

"What are your plans for today?" asked Damien.

"We'll, I'm supposed to meet Shanice at the mall, and she claims that she has some juicy news. What are you going to do? Do you want to come with us?" She offered.

"No, I'll probably go catch up on some work or something."

They sat and ate in comfortable silence, relishing the private time they had together. Even when the odds were against them they still prevailed. She cherished waking in the morning with Damien at her side. It felt so right being with him. The damage done in the beginning of the relationship allowed them to build a stronger foundation for the future. Mahogany slowly began to trust Damien again, but she would not allow him to completely have a hold on her heart. She forgave him and moved past his infidelity. They were together now and that is all that mattered. After eating, they retreated to their bedroom for a long session of love-making.

Mahogany spotted Shanice near the water fountain in the mall. Wearing jeans and a gray sweatshirt, she still looked like a young teenager.

"What's up," greeted Mahogany "So what is this juicy news you have?"

Looking down at the floor Shanice began to mumble, "I just don't know how to tell you this."

"What? What is it," asked Mahogany. Shanice looked as if she was about to pass out.

"Is it your mother? Is everything okay?" Shanice looked into Mahogany's concerned eyes and yelled, "Omar asked me to marry him, and we're getting married next week!" Mahogany wanted to choke her. She had been worried for nothing.

"Not funny, you really had me going there. Congratulations!!" Mahogany hugged her best friend. They've come a long way.

"When did he ask?" pumped Mahogany.

"Last night."

"My, my. So what prompted him, you guys should have been married a while ago."

"I don't know," claimed Shanice. She added nonchalantly, "It could be because I'm three months pregnant!!"

"No way! Are you serious?" Mahogany was totally caught off guard, in no way did she see this coming. She knew that they were not as closed as they used to be, with each having a significant other in their life, who had the time? Mahogany wasn't familiar with the current events in Shanice's life. Granted, she didn't even know when Shanice graduated, what really mattered was that they would always be there for one another, no matter what.

"As a heart attack!"

"Wait a minute, did you say three months? Why am I just now finding out?" she demanded. Looking sheepishly, Shanice smiled.

"Well, Omar wanted us to keep it private for a while, he wanted us to enjoy the fact that we were about to become parents."

"Whatever," reasoned Mahogany, "You should have told me!!"

She was losing her best friend.

"C'mon, let's go celebrate. I'll buy you the biggest plate of nachos we could find."

"You do know the way to my heart. You are forgiven." Grabbing her hand, Shanice led Mahogany to the Nachoria.

"Why are you two getting married so quickly?"

"Omar wants to get married, I've never wanted a big wedding, so next week it's off to the court house we go, you're going to be there right?"

"Of course, you shouldn't have to ask."

"Good, it's settled then."

"What did your mom say?" asked Mahogany.

"She's so happy that she is about to have a grandchild the only sad part is that she won't be able to make it to my wedding. She has some convention she needs to attend."

"What about your dad?"

"They're attending the convention together. It's a marriage convention that teaches couples how to handle constructive criticism without getting too emotional." Shanice reflected for a moment on the fights she witnessed as a child. Her parents were long overdue for counseling.

Mahogany let out a deep sigh. "I just can't believe you're getting married and having a baby. Now I'm going to have to share you."

"Don't worry pretty soon there will be enough of me to go around." Mahogany smiled. Life was changing right before her very eyes. Shanice pregnancy made Mahogany reevaluate her life. What was she doing with it? Nothing. It was a sad but true fact that was about to change. After eating and browsing the mall, the women retreated to their apartments, each one ready to embark on the unknown future ahead of them.

*   *   *

The wedding took place downtown at the courthouse. Shanice and Omar declared and vowed before the priest to love and honor each other until death did them part. Shanice looked angelic in her white dress, it was simple and elegant. Her hair was swept up in a French twist, which helped display, her high cheekbones. Omar rented a tuxedo. He wanted to be dressed for the occasion. The wedding was picture perfect. The only conflict that arose was Omar's refusal to wear his boutonnière.

He thought it made him look girlish. Mahogany did cry. She was happy for her friend and sad in the same way. Maybe deep down she hoped she and Damien would soon tie the knot. Was he ready for such a commitment? He was working late at the office trying to impress Mr. Russell. She was twenty years old and headed nowhere fast. Yes, she did get a promotion at work, but she did not plan on spending the rest of her life at IBM. Yesterday she called NC State to set-up an appointment with an advisor. She made up her mind to go back to college. After the wedding, Omar and Shanice departed for their honeymoon. They were going to spend the weekend at a resort up in the mountains. Mahogany wished the best of luck to the both of them. She wanted nothing but happiness for them. Omar got an entry-level job as a reporter. He would bring home twenty-seven thousand a year, not including bonuses. It looked as if they were going to make it.

*   *   *

Damn it, damn it. She was late again. Mr. Russell was going to chew her ass up and spit it out. At lunch Mahogany thought she would have plenty of time to run over to NC State, turn her registration schedule in, and return to work. Things never happen as you planned them. When she arrived at her advisor's office, there was a line at least a mile long. She couldn't just drop it off like she wanted to, without her advisor's signature she would not be able to attend any classes. So, she spent all of her lunch hour in line. She hadn't eaten anything for breakfast. It took her advisor a whole two seconds to sign Mahogany's schedule. Taking the approved schedule, Mahogany flew out of the door. Mr. Russell probably had her pink slip filled out already. Half sprinting and walking, Mahogany made it to IBM in record time. She was so hungry. She was about to get in the elevator when the vending machine in the back hallway caught her eye.

Oh yes. She could eat a candy bar or some chips, anything to stop her stomach from gnawing into her back. Ignoring the elevator, Mahogany made a mad dash to the vending machine. Spotting the sour cream and cheddar flavored chips, she quickly put her money in the machine.

She waited for the chips to drop to the bottom. They never did. The demon in her came out. Bending down on the floor she tried maneuvering her arm inside of the machine to make the chips fall from the last row. She almost had them. Her fingertips were touching the bag.

Almost, almost.

She was interrupted by the sound of a man clearing his throat.

"Excuse me, ma'am can I help you?"

Horrified, Mahogany used all the dignity she could muster to stand up. In front of her, a very amused man stared down at her.

"I wasn't trying to steal anything, my chips got suck and..."

"Mahogany? Are you Mahogany Fox?"

"Yes."

"You don't remember me? I'm Jake. Jake Reeves, we used to go to high school together." She still looked confused. "Remember, I sat two rows away from you in Mr. McMurtrey class?" He saw her light bulb come on.

"Yes! You had red hair, what happened to it?"

He rubbed his hair, "As you can see, I've changed." And change he did thought Mahogany. No longer was he the scrawny boy she and Shanice used to make fun of. He had developed into a nice looking young man. His red hair had turned into brown causing his green eyes to stand out even more. While his shoulders filled his suit out in a way Mahogany would not believe unless she saw it for herself.

"So what are you doing here in Raleigh?" she questioned.

"Oh, I work for the Raleigh Vending Department. I prosecute people who attempt to rob poor helpless vending machines." Mahogany laughed, hoping that he was joking.

"Cute. Seriously, what are you doing now?"

"I work here."

"You do? How long have you've been working here? I've never seen you."

He scratched his head, "Oh, I've been here for two, almost three months."

"What department are you in?" IBM was a big place, but not that big.

"Receivables, I handle all the money."

Mahogany looked at her watch, a panic stricken look to crossed her face.

"Oh, shit. I'm in trouble. I must go, Jake. Look, I'll be seeing you around. Maybe we'll do lunch?"

Jake watched her run off towards the elevators. It sure was nice to see someone form home. He would make it a point to meet up with her. Mahogany Fox. Who would have thought he would ever see her again?

Chapter 8

The mall was packed. A person could not walk for a second without someone bumping into them. No matter the time or season, the Raleigh Civic Mall always managed to have a crowd. Aware that Shanice was due to have her baby any day now, Mahogany figured it was high time she bought Shanice's baby some outfits. Every time she tried to purchase something Shanice told her it was bad luck to buy baby clothes before the baby was born. An old wives tale, which she claimed had validity. The doctors told her and Omar that she was having a little girl. Mahogany, busy with work and college, now had time to shop for her goddaughter. Mahogany could not help but laugh as Shanice tried to keep up with her. Poor baby, she looked as if she was going to explode. Her face was so full, not to mention the seventy-pounds she gained during her pregnancy.

Better her than me.

Mahogany held up a pretty pink outfit. "Do you like this?" Looking at the outfit Shanice knew her daughter would be lucky if she could wear the outfit more than once.

"Yea, let's get it." She was tired and ready to go home. Why did she agree to come with her? She detested the mall. She had a headache from just looking at the "sale" and "clearance" signs.

After paying for the outfit, Mahogany surveyed the mall for other potential shopping possibilities.

"Shanice, what do you think God thinks of us?"

"What do you mean?" wondered Shanice. Mahogany always had pondered strange psychological aspects.

"You know, about all of the stuff we've done."

"He's probably looking down on us thinking, 'What in the world are they doing' or 'Here we go again.'" Mahogany laughed. "Well, you really don't have anything to worry about since you're married."

"That's not true. Remember the stuff I did before I met Omar?" She shivered remembering.

"Yea, the stuff I'm doing now with Damien."

Mahogany put her head down and let out a deep sigh, "Come Judgment Day, God is going to have us sit down and watch a video tape of our life." Mahogany cringed. She could not imagine herself with God watching the most sinful things she did in life. "Oh, no! I would cover my eyes," screamed Mahogany.

"God would be right there asking you, 'Now tell me child, what was going through your mind as you did that?"

"And I would tell him the same thing I used to tell my momma, 'I don't know.'"

Both women collapsed in fits of laughter.

"Mahogany, now you know if your mom didn't buy that lie, what makes you even think that God will?"

"I don't know," reasoned Mahogany. "Maybe He will look inside our hearts to figure out why we sinned in the first place."

"I guess that's a good way to look at it. Now let's go home, my feet are killing me."

Leaving the mall, Mahogany couldn't get their conversation out of her head. Although, they were joking, it really did bother her that she and Damien had not taken any steps to fully commit to each other. Hopefully, that will change.

* * *

"I'm not ready," Damien explained to Mahogany.

"What do you mean, 'you're not ready?' We've been together for almost two years, how much more "ready" do you need to be?" He was still giving her the same bullshit story.

"Why do we have to be married? Why can't we just be together?"

Did he honestly think that less of her? It was fine with him to fuck her without a commitment. No strings or ties for Damien Andrews. He needed to be able to up and leave whenever he chose to. Never needing to look back. Things couldn't be more perfect for him.

"You're fine just living here?" she demanded. Mahogany waved her hands towards the cramped apartment.

"Yes," declared Damien. "I love being here with you, just the two of us. I mean, we love each other, isn't that enough?"

"No, it's not." The phone rang interrupting their charged discussion.

"Hello? Hello?" A resounding "click" echoed in her ear. This was the third time someone had called her apartment and hung-up. It was obvious that Damien was fucking around on her. She looked at him.

"So how long have you been cheating on me?"

"What? I'm not. Why would you ask me that?"

"Because someone has called her the last couple of days hanging up on me."

"That's no reason to accuse me of anything!"

The more defensive he got, the less she believed him.

"I'm not accusing, I'm just stating the facts. I find it interesting that every time I pick up the phone someone hangs up in my face."

"Don't be upset with me for your paranoia," he demanded. He was tired of being accused of things Mahogany "thought" she knew. She never gave him the benefit of the doubt. Until she actually caught him doing something, he didn't want to hear her mouth.

"Fine, I'll be upset with you because of the truth. The truth is that you are fucking around and whoever you are fucking around with is giving me the usual courtesy call to let me know."

"Let you know what, Mahogany? I'm not doing anything." Mahogany's instinct was telling her the contrary. He was doing something, she would find out sooner or later. She needed to clear her mind. It wasn't everyday that the man she was in love with told her that she was good enough to screw but not good enough to be his wife.

"I'm going for a walk."

"Mahogany, don't leave. Let's talk about this. Forget about the phone call mess, I want you to understand how I feel about marriage. I do believe in it. I'm just not ready for it." Mahogany could tell that he was telling the truth. She just wasn't ready to accept it. Feeling lost she left the apartment.

After closing the door to her apartment, something in the corridor caught her eye.

She nearly stopped breathing, should she call Damien? A lady's body was crouched down in the corner. Her brown hair covered the majority of her face, but Mahogany could tell that her face was beaten to a pulp. She rushed over to help.

"Ma'am, are you okay? Do you need me to call an ambulance?" She could tell that the lady was in great pain. She saw blood oozing from her right temple. Fumbling in her purse, Mahogany found some Kleenex. She awkwardly tried to dab the blood away. While looking at the lady's face Mahogany's hand began to shake violently. She recognized her face.

"Dawn?"

Chapter 9

Mahogany listened in disbelief as Dawn recounted the abuse she experienced at Shane's hands. Drunken tirades, violent outburst, and verbal abuse. After hearing Dawn recount the events she understood why so many women stayed in abusive relationships. Shane was nice, friendly, and smart enough to make Dawn believe the abuse she experienced at his hands was her fault. She spent years being a victim. Fearful for her life, Dawn begged Mahogany not to call an ambulance. She did not want to leave a trail.

"How did you find me?"

"Your mother. Two weeks ago, I ran into her and she gave me your address." Dawn paused for a moment, "It was good that she did, I don't know what I would have done if she hadn't. After he beat me I just got in the car and drove. I had to get away." Mahogany rubbed Dawn bruised hands.

"I'm happy that you did. Damien should be back any minute with the first aid kit." Dawn managed to smile through her busted lips. "He's cute where did you meet him?"

"At work, we saw each other and it was love or lust at first sight. Which ever you prefer?"

"Does he treat you well?"

"He does the best that he can," Mahogany answered. "So is there anything new happening in Idaho? Every time I speak to my mom she claims nothing new has occurred over the last few years."

"She's right," agreed Dawn. "The only thing that makes the news is if someone stabs a potato. Do you miss it?"

"No, not really. Idaho is so dead compared to North Carolina. Another cool thing about North Carolina is that more than one black person lives here." Dawn grinned.

Mahogany looked the same as she did in high school. Gone was the naïve look she carried in her eyes. Dawn did not know how to explain it, Mahogany had the same beautiful face and same gorgeous smile. She just looked more mature. Her friend that helped her pull pranks was gone and replaced with a headstrong woman.

Hearing the door close Mahogany jumped up, "That must be Damien." Mahogany returned with the bandages and ointment. After bandaging her up, Mahogany ordered Dawn to get some sleep. Rubbing her hair, Mahogany couldn't imagine the Hell she had been through. She would do whatever it took to protect her.

Later on during the week Mahogany called Shanice from work to fill her in on the latest with Dawn. Not even a full term pregnancy could prevent her from checking on Dawn. Interrupting her thoughts were the loud voices of Bruce and the cleaning lady, not again.

"You did it! I know you did it." Bruce's loud country voice vibrated off the walls.

"Me no do nothing, leave me alone," the cleaning lady tried in vain to escape Bruce's wrath.

"I know you threw away my coffee, I saw ya do it!"

"You no know nothing. Move, move out of my way." Once again, she tried to push her cleaning cart past Bruce.

"I will not move out of your way! I want you to give me a $1.10 so I can buy myself another cup of coffee!"

Pointing her finger in his face she said quietly, "Me no give you shit." Bruce's face turned beat red. Mahogany saw Jake witnessing the circus with an amused grin on his face. Yea, it was about to get ugly.

Bruce hunched down so that he was eye to eye with the cleaning lady. He wanted her to comprehend every word that he was about to say. Looking squarely in her face Bruce shouted, "You're nothin' but a mother-fucker!"

Feeling that his job was completed, he stormed off in a huff. Smiling, the cleaning lady sang an Asian medley. Barely able to restrain his laughter Jake collapsed at Mahogany's desk.

"Man, that guy is smoking some serious crack." He wiped the tears rolling down his cheeks. Mahogany struggled to catch her breath. Deciding to imitate Bruce, she gathered her composure and whispered, "You're nothin' but a Mother-Fucker!" They fell out laughing again.

"Stop it," begged Jake. "I can't take anymore." Mahogany relented. Her stomach couldn't take much more.

"What is that guy problem?" wondered Jake.

"He's been like that for as long as I've known him." Jake looked at Mahogany as if he was seeing her for the first time.

"You know, I don't think that I laughed that hard since someone got her paper changed in Mr. McMurtrey class in high school."

"I think it was funnier when someone got their truck toilet papered," snickered Mahogany. "Who could forget you and that eye soar you had as a car? We toilet papered it just to make it look better."

"Nope, you win hands down. I would die from embarrassment if a teacher read aloud anything I wrote about sex. Who cares if you didn't write it, Mr. McMurtrey thought you did," he said.

"Why, does the subject of sex make you uncomfortable?"

"No, not at all."

All of sudden, Mahogany felt Jake was looking through her soul. Breaking the tension, Jake asked, "Do you want to go to lunch? With all the commotion going on I forgot the main reason why I came up here."

"Sure, what time?" If Damien did not like it, great. She had completed her mission of pissing him off.

"How's your mom? I got the vague impression that she didn't like me."

"She liked you, she just thought you were out of my league."

A page for Mahogany sounded through the building.

What happened? Mahogany rushed to her office where Mr. Russell waited with a note in his hand. This was it he was going to fire her. Couldn't he just write her up for what ever she had done?

"Mahogany, the hospital just called. It seems a Mrs. Shanice Berry has given birth to a little girl. Seven pounds, six ounces." Mahogany was out the door in a flash. Shanice should have called her to let know that she was in labor. She made it to the hospital in record time. She stood in the doorway watching Shanice nurse her newborn baby.

"What did you name her?"

"Shante Olivia." Mahogany could tell that she was groggy from the medicine.

"She is so tiny and gorgeous, where's the proud papa?"

"On the payphone down the hall, calling his family I'm sure."

"She looks exactly like Omar. She has his eyes, nose, and even his mouth."

Shanice agreed, "You know what they say, 'Women do all the hard work and the men shall reap the benefits.'"

"I will assume that statement as true. When did you go into labor and why didn't you call me?"

"I was on my way to check on Dawn when the pains started hitting me. They were coming from the left and the right. The pains never let up, so I turned back around and went home. Luckily Omar was still there because ten minutes after we arrived at the hospital, I had Shante."

Touching her godchild on the head, Mahogany abated. "I forgive you for not calling me, but next time I'm not having it. So did it hurt?"

"I could lie to you and tell you that it didn't, but it did."

"On a scale of one to ten."

Shanice shook her head in disagreement, "I would give it at least a fifty."

"You must be joking. It couldn't hurt that bad, it didn't hurt at all going in."

"Trust me, Mahogany, the birth pains more than make-up for that moment of pleasure." Mahogany groaned, women suffered so much unnecessary pain, cramps, and labor, what's next?

The nurse entered the hospital room. "Excuse me, Shanice, but we need to run some test on you and your baby."

"Are you going to wait around?" asked Shanice.

"No, I'm going to check on Dawn since I have the rest of the day off."

"Alright, tell her that I'm sorry that I couldn't make it, I had more important things to do."

Mahogany laughed, "Yea, I'll explain it to her."

Once outside Mahogany realized that she forgot to tell Damien that she was leaving work. The more she was around Damien the less she cared about pleasing him. On the drive home, she continued to think about it. They were at a point in their relationship where something desperately needed to change. Opening the door to her apartment she saw that Dawn was still asleep.

"Mahogany?"

"Yes, Dawn. I thought that you were asleep, how are you feeling?"

"Fine, the best I could expect." Mahogany watched as Dawn wrung her hands together.

"What? What is it?"

"Would you mind if I were to stay here for a while? Just until I get my feet back on the ground."

"Of course, of course you can, Dawn. Take as much time as you need. You've been through a horrible ordeal. You are welcome to stay as long as you need to."

"Thank you, you won't even know that I'm here."

"Well, it's pretty hard to ignore someone who snores as loud as you do!" Looking at Dawn's stricken face, Mahogany told her that she was only joking. With Dawn living in Raleigh life just got a little bit more interesting. Knowing Dawn, Mahogany hoped that it was for the better.

Chapter 10

Fucking bitch. He was going to get her. She had no idea that he was getting close, which was fine with him. He planned on making the bitch paying for what she did to him. No one could save her from him. He hated her just as much as he loved her. Just the thought of her existence made him sick. It was his destiny to eliminate her presence from this world. The bitch did not deserve to live. He glanced at the pictures of her plastered on the wall. She was laughing at him, he could tell by looking in her eyes.

Beautiful eyes of the devil.

He loved her. He loved to hate her. The only thing that bothered him was her beautiful face. He really didn't want to cut it.

He was getting closer and closer. When the time was right, he would kill her. Let her think that she won. The game was not over. All those years of her constantly baiting him would not go unpunished. He had to strike her down. When the time is right, he would have her crimson blood spilling in his hands, running over his fingers.

Only when the time was right. Let her think that she got away. He would get her. That was definite.

Chapter 11

What was she thinking? How could she marry a man after only knowing him for a year? Should she file for divorce? No one would understand, as far as everyone was concerned Omar was a fine, decent man. But this coming home straight from work and playing the PlayStation nonstop was old. Very old.

Shante would be seven months old in a couple of weeks and Omar had not taken Shanice out for a night on the town since she had the baby. Now that they had a baby he expected her to sit at home and be bored. She could not, no refused to be a housewife. To make matters worse, he hardly did anything with Shante. She had to practically beg him just to feed his own daughter. She assumed fatherhood did not come naturally to him. Each time she suggested that they do something together, he would find an excuse just so he could stay home and play his beloved Play Station.

She was restless.

It wasn't like they did not have a babysitter. Mahogany offered on more than one occasion to watch Shante. Even their neighbor Yasmine had offered to baby-sit. She offered her services one day when she saw Shanice struggling with some groceries. Explaining that if she and Omar wanted to go out, give her a call. Yasmine's young and carefree attitude made her seem trustworthy. There was no reason for Omar's boring behavior. Even the sex was different. How did a two-hour session get cut to fifteen minutes? Shanice was fed-up.

Sensing her unhappiness, Yasmine invited her to a get together tonight and she was going. Omar hardly noticed Shanice getting ready for the party, when he did notice, he still did not want to go.

"I'll be next door," yelled Shanice. "If Shante awakes she has two bottles in the refrigerator."

"Alright, baby." Omar tried executing a combination move on the Play station controller and failed. He could not figure out how to beat the computer in *Mortal Kombat*. The computer knew every move he made before he made it. He was determined to beat the game.

Shanice rang the doorbell. By all the cars in the driveway she could tell that the party was well underway. Yasmine opened the door looking fabulous. Wearing a skin tight beige dress that hugged every curve, her unique dark skin made Shanice think that Yasmine probably was one of the most beautiful women she had ever seen.

"Come in, Shanice. Let me introduce you to my friends."

As Yasmine and Shanice circulated among the guest, Shanice could tell that Yasmine's beauty held her company under a hypnotic spell. She seemed oblivious to the stares, yet Shanice could tell that she secretly enjoyed knowing people wanted her. If Shanice had a body like Yasmine, she no doubt would use it to get a reaction.

After her third drink, Shanice let the alcohol vibrate through her veins. She felt more relaxed than she had in months. Someone had slipped Babyface in the CD player.

Babyface undoubtedly made people get a little freaky. The whole mood and frequency of the party changed with his voice crooning throughout the house. Shanice thought it would be best if she left the party. The room was already spinning. She had to find Yasmine to let her know that she was leaving. She spotted her in the kitchen.

"Yasmine. I'm gonna leave now, thanks for inviting me."

"You're more than welcomed, Shanice. Let me walk you to the door."

Grabbing her hand Yasmine led Shanice towards the door, but instead of going outside Yasmine led her upstairs to her room.

"Where are we going?" asked Shanice.

"Upstairs. Just follow me," said Yasmine. "I just needed to escape from all that noise." They sat on Yasmine's bed. Babyface's "Whip Appeal" bellowed up the stairs. Suddenly, the room got smaller, intimate.

"Thanks for coming by Shanice."

"Sure, no problem. I was literally dying to get out of the house. I was getting sick of the same old routine." The liquor made Shanice's tongue very loose. "Omar doesn't want to do anything anymore, he's happy with his video games. I need something different, not the same…I'm not happy with my life right now."

"What do you think you need to make yourself happy?"

"Spontaneity. Omar is predictable, I need him to be unpredictable."

"Unpredictable, how?"

"Surprise kisses, him grabbing my hand and taking me off so we can go for a walk, just the two of us like we used to…not much, simple things every wife asks for."

"That doesn't seem like a lot. I don't know why he isn't supplying you with your every want and need."

Careful not to frighten her, Yasmine grabbed Shanice by the face and kissed her. A kiss Shanice felt all the way to her belly, thoughts ran through her mind.

What was she doing? Why wasn't she pulling away? What was wrong with her?

Yasmine sensed Shanice's confusion, she whispered in her ear, "It's okay. Just let it flow."

The scary thing was that Shanice wanted to "let it flow." It was as if Yasmine turned into a bright flame beckoning Shanice to get burnt. Yasmine kissed her again, only it was deeper, more passionate.

Shanice's brain screamed. She needed to stop, but instead she started returning Yasmine kisses with a vengeance. She did not want to stop. The unknown intrigued her. By having a taste of the forbidden, Shanice desperately wanted more. Their tongues slipped and slided out of each other mouth. Yasmine slowly lowered Shanice onto the bed, covering her with her body. Yasmine's mouth attacked her mouth and neck. Even trying to suck Shanice's firm nipples through her clothes.

"Shanice! Shanice, are you up here?" Omar came into the room and turned the lights on. "What the hell? Why are you guys up here in the dark?"

Jumping up from the bed, Shanice explained, "We just needed to get away from the noise, that's all." Omar could smell the alcohol on her breath from where he was standing.

"Girl, c'mon. Let's go, you should have been at home." Shanice followed Omar down the stairs, never looking back at Yasmine.

What had she done?

Chapter 12

Life finally turned around for Dawn. Not only did Mahogany allow Dawn to stay as long as she needed to, she helped Dawn put her resume together. Dawn was now employed at *Stones Uncovered*, a local detective agency. Pretty soon she would have enough money for her own apartment. Not that she did not like staying with Mahogany and Damien, she just felt like she was intruding.

Dawn took no special care preparing for work. Mr. Peck, her boss, really did not care what time she got there, just as long as she was there. It seems he had bad luck keeping help. His bad breath and overbearing attitude were both powerful deterrents in running off future employees. Dawn discovered that working for a detective agency had its advantages. She was surprised by the amount of dirt they were able to find on people. Amazing, she always heard, "what's done in the dark comes to light." Mahogany came storming in the apartment looking like she just got into a fight. Dawn could tell that she was livid with anger.

"Tell me why did I, Mahogany Fox, just got stopped on the campus of NC State by some chicken head who claimed that she was Damien's girlfriend. His girlfriend of the past six months!" Dawn stared in silence. She could tell that Mahogany was hurt. Her voice was strong and gritty, but her soul seemed dejected.

"Tell me!" she demanded.

Never one to lie, Dawn offered, "Didn't you say that when you first met Damien he was with someone else? Maybe it's a cycle."

"Dawn, shut-up! Will you please be quiet? I really don't need to hear that shit right now!" Mahogany sat down on the couch. "Why did I have to fall in love with him? Things would be so much easier if he was a horrible person and terrible lover, but Damien he just…"

"Mahogany, we both know that if you love someone you don't hurt them. That's the last thing you do."

"I can't do this anymore. I've already been through this shit. I refuse to go through it again. I was a fool for trusting him the first time and the second time, there won't be a third." Looking around the apartment, Mahogany took a deep breath. "Dawn, if you knew all the shit I've been through for this boy."

"You said it right, 'boy.' He still has a great deal of growing up to do. He's still playing the game, all men do."

"But why? Why can't they just be faithful? If they want to start seeing someone else, fine. Be a man and tell us so. They say women play too many games, where do we learn them? Relationships could last forever, if everyone quit speaking with a forked tongue." Dawn put Mahogany hands within hers, "Why didn't he tell me?"

"Because that would spoil the game, Mahogany. He's still at the batter's plate waiting on the next piece of ass he could hit."

"Help me pack up Damien's stuff, he isn't staying one more night here."

"Are you serious? Where is he going to go?"

"I'm sure that chicken head is more than willing to take him in."

They spent an hour gathering Damien's belongings. Mahogany asked Dawn to leave when she heard Damien come home. This was something she needed to handle on her own. Upon entering the apartment a sense of Déjà vu overcame Damien. He saw his belongings at the door.

"Mahogany? What's going on?"

"Nothing."

He could tell that she was pissed. Her left eyebrow stuck straight up.

"Then why is all of my stuffed packed?"

He honestly did not have a clue. Looking into his eyes, Mahogany could tell that he knew he was caught.

"I ran into Renee. Do you know a Renee?"

Mahogany listened as Damien turned a "no" into a "yes," then how he and Renee were only friends or how she was jealous of Mahogany and she was just trying to make her mad. Mahogany didn't even ask how this Renee knew of her in the first place. She knew that it would lead to more lies. Lies, she did not need to hear right now. The sooner Damien Andrews was out of her life the better off she would be.

"Mahogany, let's just discuss this. I do not want to leave like this."

"How do you want to leave? You want to leave making sure everyone knows that I am a fool?"

"No, Mahogany. Please, baby, I'll do anything you say."

"Really? Call Renee up. I want to speak with her. Let's get to the bottom of this." Damien struggled to find words, but nothing came out of his mouth. "Good-bye, Damien."

He finally left after claiming he would make it up to her, he loved her. Blah, blah, blah. Mahogany had listened to enough of his mess. She went into her bedroom and laid down. Damien's scent was everywhere. And then she did something she hadn't done in a long time, she cried herself to sleep. She hated Damien. He had put her through so much. First thing tomorrow, she would go down to the health department and get tested for everything. There's no telling what Damien might have given her. Since he was a firm believer in sticking himself in every female known to man.

✶   ✶   ✶

Shanice's hormones were raging. Everything that could go wrong did. Shante was teething, she did not have any teething medicine, Omar had no idea what time he would be home, and dinner was burnt. She rested her head against the refrigerator.

Deep down, she knew what the problem was or should she say "who" the problem was.

Yasmine.

Since the party, Shanice could not get her out of her head. She blamed everything that happened that night on alcohol. But could she blame the alcohol on the emotions she felt? They did say that alcohol was a stimulant. Why was she lying to herself? She could not believe that she was physically and emotionally attracted to another female.

There! She admitted it. It boggled her mind just thinking about it. She never looked at women that way. Yet, there was something about Yasmine. They had not spoken since that night. Every time Yasmine called, she would let the machine answer. She was not one to temp fate. Shante's incessant crying triggered Shanice from her thoughts. Where was Omar with the medicine? The telephone rang. Maybe that was him.

"Hello?"

"Can you meet me at the St. Night's Hotel?" Shanice's heart dropped. Yasmine obviously believed in tempting fate.

"Where at?"

"I'll be in room 326. Will you be there?"

"Yes."

"I'll see you around 9:30pm?"

"Alright."

Shanice hung up the telephone. Boy was the devil busy.

Omar did manage to come early with the teething medicine. He apologized for not being able to come sooner. "What happened to dinner?" His innocent question provided the opportunity of escape for Shanice.

"What do you mean what happened to dinner? I've been here all day trying my best and you step in here demanding things. Tell me, have you been here all day with Shante, trying to take care of her?"

"No, no, I haven't and I'm not trying to down play your role as a parent or a wife. If you accidentally burnt dinner that's fine, let's order out. It's no big deal."

Shanice was undeterred, "That's where you are wrong! It is a big deal when you question my integrity or me. I don't need this."

"Need what?" Now he was getting angry. "What are you talking about?"

"I'm talking about everything. You, your Play Station, and you not paying attention to me."

"If you got a problem with me being in my house, playing my Play Station, deal with it!"

"I will." Shanice pushed past Omar and grabbed her purse and left.

She had a date tonight.

Shanice was still on a rush from the argument with Omar when she knocked on room 326.

"Come in, Shanice. I've been waiting for you. I didn't think you would come."

"Why did you call me?" Shanice hoped that Yasmine had a valid reason. She did not think that she would be able to refrain from giving into her passion.

"You already know why."

Yasmine placed Shanice's face between both of hands. "And if you say that you don't, you would be lying to yourself. Let me," Yasmine kissed Shanice on the lips, "Show you why you came." Each kiss Yasmine applied to Shanice ultimately caused a deep throbbing between Shanice's legs. They stood against the door. Yasmine kissed Shanice like she had never been kissed before. Yasmine main focus was Shanice's mouth, lips, and tongue. She wanted it all. Every last drop.

Using her hand Yasmine unzipped Shanice's pants and inserted her fingers inside of Shanice.

"No," whispered Shanice, her legs felt as if they were about to collapse from underneath her.

"Yes, Oh Yes, I want you to give it to me, Shanice."

Shanice wanted to, she kissed Yasmine back. She needed this, whatever this was. She wanted it, craved it, and desired it. Yasmine pushed Shanice down onto the bed all the while keeping her fingers moving inside of her. Yasmine used her other hand to undress Shanice. Taking her breast into her mouth, Yasmine sucked Shanice's nipple. She needed more of her. If she could drink her, she would. Yasmine kissed her way down her stomach and spread Shanice's legs apart with both her hands. Her legs shaking with want.

"Please, please," begged Shanice.

"Oh, now you want something from me? I thought you told me "no."

Yasmine kissed Shanice's inner thighs, taking her time she moved to the outer section of her thighs. Pretending to ignore what begged for her attention. Shanice grabbed a hand full of sheets in her impatience.

"What do you want?" Yasmine teased.

"Your mouth. Your mouth."

"Where? Here?" Yasmine tantalized Shanice's clit with her warm breath. She knew that Shanice could not hold out much longer. She forcefully put her hot mouth on Shanice's flesh. Damn, she loved the smell of her. Yasmine let her wicked tongue play Shanice.

"Oh shit, this shit is good, don't stop. What the fuck, ohhh, I can't stop…oh, oh, oh!" shouted Shanice.

Huge waves of orgasms crashed through her body. Never had that happened to her. Never. Gasping for air, she couldn't help but wonder. What had she gotten herself into?

Chapter 13

Mahogany felt like crap. She had sex with Damien. The only reason she wasn't beating herself up for it was because she made him wear a condom. No harm done. She could not stay away from him. In reality, she had invested three years of her life into Damien. She had put blood, sweat, and tears into building something. She would be damn if she did not get anything in return. It wasn't that easy to stop wanting someone. Luckily, he left before Dawn returned from work. Lately, she'd been so judgmental. Mahogany decided to call Shanice, she hadn't spoken to her in a couple of days.

"Hello?"
"Hey, girl what's up?"
"Nothing much."
"Damien just left."
"What was he doing there? Mahogany, did you guys sleep together?" Shanice sounded like a disappointed mother.
"I know, I know. What can I say? I'm weak, but I did use a condom."
"Well good for you."
"So, what's happening with you?"
"You wouldn't believe me if I told you."
"Believe what? Shanice?"

It was killing her. She had to tell someone, anyone, anybody! She held her secret in for a week.

"Now what I'm about to tell you, you have to promise not to tell anyone."

"I promise," vowed Mahogany.

"Say honest to God," demanded Shanice.

Taking a deep breath, Shanice blurted, "I had sex with a woman."

"Honest, Shanice, now tell me," replied Mahogany.

Mahogany stopped breathing. She looked at the telephone like it was to blame for what she heard.

"What did you say?"

"You heard me. I slept with another woman."

She had known Shanice since, since, ever. Not one time did she notice any lesbian tendencies.

"When? With who?"

"My neighbor. I can't believe I did this."

"What kind of neighborhood do you live in? This is pretty heavy. Why? Don't you like Omar? Men? Penis?"

"Yes, I like men. It's just something about her. I think she is the devil in disguise."

"I guess so. So what exactly did you two do?"

"What do you mean, 'what did we do?'"

"Did she use tools or what?"

"No, she did not. I can't believe I'm telling you this. We did the usual things that people do when they have sex."

"Oh." By that 'oh' Shanice knew Mahogany would never fully understand. "Shanice, I still can't believe…"

"I know, neither can I."

Mahogany did not know what to say. It seems that both her and Shanice were at a point in their life when their ship was sinking fast. If they were smart, they would signal S.O.S. She wondered about God. What was He thinking now? Both women held their heads down in shame. They were on a one-way path to destruction.

Chapter 14

He was looking at her ass.

"Lt. Peck, I would appreciate if you placed your eyes somewhere else besides my ass." He smiled guiltily, "You can't blame me for admiring fine artwork."

"Yes, I can. So could my lawyer if you don't stop it." Just the thought of his grimy mind thinking of her made Dawn sick.

"It's no wonder that your previous help never stuck around. You're just like a dirty old man."

"Now that's not true. I'm a sweet and innocent man." Dawn watched his greasy lips form a smile.

"Yea, innocent like a hooker on a Friday night."

"Oh, like you are a goody too shoes? I doubt that very seriously."

"Why is that?" It sounded like an accusation.

"Well, if you really want to know. I don't like women who could give away their kids like a Christmas present and go through life as if nothing happened."

Not a day had gone by without Dawn thinking about her child. She had delivered a baby boy. But everyone, including Shane thought it was best that she give him up for adoption. Dawn didn't want to, but she was young and afraid. She briefly had a chance to see her child. When he was born, the nurse permitted Dawn to hold her son. He was perfect, dark curly hair and mocha colored skin. Her parents were disgraced by her pregnancy. They refused to help her raise a bi-racial child; even it was their own grandchild. The embarrassment they would face was more important than Dawn's child.

She had listened to them.

After the nurse removed her son from her arms, Dawn suffered from emptiness. An emptiness that in no way could be filled until she had her son back. He would be three years old. He had no idea how much his mother loved and wanted him. What other options did she have at the time? Now this son-of-bitch had the nerve to throw it in her face.

"Don't you ever mention my child! You are not even worthy to think about him. How did you find out? Who told you?"

Lt. Peck shrugged his shoulders, like invading Dawn's personal life was an every day occurrence.

"I hired you, you didn't expect me to run a criminal check?"

"Yea, but in my personal life?"

He defended himself, "It's your life. When you work for me your life becomes a part of my life."

Dawn was really angry with herself. What Lt. Peck said was true. How could she have given away her baby? It was a question she asked herself every single day. Lt. Peck was still rambling, "You need to do it too. Whoever is in your life needs to be checked friend or no friend. Better safe than sorry."

"I trust my friends, which is something you ought to try." She waited until he left before she started crying. She would begin a search for her son.

* * *

"Mahogany Fox speaking, how can I help you?"

"Hello Mahogany, this is Shane. Have you heard from Dawn?"

"How did you get this number?"

"Everyone knows that you work for some big hotshot company. It wasn't that hard finding out where, I'm not a dummy."

"Listen, I would really love to chat, but I gotta go."

"Have you heard from Dawn?"

"No, why."

"Because I can't find her anywhere. Mahogany, I would really hate it if you are lying to me."

"Are you threatening me, Shane? Does that make you feel like a man when you threaten a woman?"

"Just tell me if you've heard from Dawn."

"No, I haven't and even if I did I wouldn't tell you. Do not call here again."

Chapter 15

Look at her smiling at him. Laughing. Why did she keep looking at him that way? Did she want him? After all this time he knew she still wanted him. Well, it was too late. She sealed her fate a long time ago. Now, she was speaking to him, begging him to say something. He pretended to be rational. What he really wanted to tell her was "good-bye" when he finally killed her. She shouldn't have been allowed to live this long. It was part of his plan. The longer he let her live, the safer she felt. Time was on his side. Not hers. He smiled at her. Yes, she would get what she had coming to her.

Smile, bitch, smile.

Remembering the pain she made him suffer caused his hands to ache from wanting to choke her. He continued to smile and laugh with her.

Time was on his side.

Chapter 16

Things were great. It had been a while since Mahogany could even picture her life trouble free. Work was great and her personal life was calm, provided that she stop slipping on Damien's dick every once in a while. She had needs like everyone else did. This evening she and Jake were gathering decorations for an upcoming office party.

"So what happened between you and Damien?" Mahogany looked up as if looking to God for an answer.

"I don't know, we fell out of love or we never were in love."

"Are you still in love with him?"

Mahogany smiled, "I know that I will always love him, but I'm not in love with him." Jake grabbed her hand, "I don't understand how he could let you go and I'm not just saying that. You seem like an easy person to love and stay in love with."

"Thanks for the compliment. I do believe that I am an easy person to love."

"Is that an invitation?" Sensing her embarrassment Jake covered, "Hey, I was joking. I didn't mean to make you feel awkward."

"It's fine, Jake. It's just that I was caught off guard. I never looked at you in that way before. I'm not saying it's repulsive, it's just something that I never thought of."

"Forget it, it's not big deal. Now c'mon, let's finish up with these decorations."

Mahogany wasn't honest, she had thought of Jake as a potential lover. She just did not want to give him the wrong signals. Maybe they could hook-up later. Maybe.

* * *

"No, Dawn."

"Why not? You've always wanted to."

"That was years ago. People change." They were sitting at Mahogany's apartment doing absolutely nothing. It seemed to be the same routine every day after work. Come home, watch TV, and sleep. Dawn found an ad in the newspaper about auditions for the play "Ghost." She firmly believed that the role of Oda May Brown had Mahogany's name written all over it.

"Let's go. We're not doing anything here." Dawn continued reading from the paper, "Open auditions begin at 7:30pm. Mahogany, we still have time. Let's go!" She got up, yanking Mahogany's hand.

"Dawn, do you know how long it's been since I've acted?"

"You need to do this, do something."

"No, I'm not doing it."

Mahogany's protest fell on deaf ears even as Dawn dragged her from the apartment. They arrived downtown. Signs were everywhere leading to the audition. The auditions were taking place at the Shrine Coliseum.

"I don't think that this was a good idea at all."

"Well, you're not here to think, but to act."

Dawn and Mahogany watched as each hopeful actress entered the auditorium room. Her palms were already sweating. It had been a long time since she had a rush like this. It felt good. When name her name was called, she jumped. Pushing aside her fears and nervousness, Mahogany entered the room while Dawn waited outside. The room was cramped. She assumed it was a storage room because there were boxes everywhere. Two figures sat beside the director. All three had looks of expectation on their face. Memorizing from the script they given her, she began her cold reading. After reading the first word something came over her. Her voice, gestures, and her body changed into the character. Whoopi look out, she was in the zone. After she completed her scene the obscure director said the usual, "Thank you. We'll call you in a couple of weeks." Then looking at her name on the sheet, he asked if she had a head shot?"

"No, I don't."

Shaking his head, he murmured, "Thanks." Mahogany left the room. What did that mean? Did she get the part? Did they like her?

"How did it go?" She could tell that Mahogany liked the audition.

"It went pretty well. I can't tell if they thought I sucked or what."

"You did fine, just fine." Mahogany gave Dawn a quick hug.

"Thanks for making me do this, I needed it. She hadn't felt this happy in a long time."

"Your welcome, Mahogany. We must learn to have more fun."

"Yes, we do," agreed Mahogany.

Both went home content. Sitting at home on a Saturday night definitely was a thing of the past. It they did not change, life would surely pass them by.

*   *   *

Shanice was whipped. A pitiful fact that she was too blind to see. The more time she spent with Yasmine, the more she detested Omar. Her marriage was in shambles. As a result of her behavior, Omar didn't even come home from work and when he did Shanice would get a barrage of hang-ups in her ear. She was fucking someone, he was fucking someone, and she had no idea when it would stop.

Did she want it to?

She was in love with Yasmine and willing to sacrifice her marriage. It was the reason why she was packing her and Shante's clothes. Yasmine wanted her to move in with her, which was fine with Shanice. She could not stand to live one more minute with Omar. She disliked his presence. Everything he said or did seem to irritate her nerves.

"What the hell are you doing?" Omar had decided to come home for lunch to pick up an overnight bag. The last thing he expected to see was his wife moving out.

"Packing a bag. What does it look like?" She continued to put items in her bag like he wasn't even there.

"Where do you think you're taking my daughter?"

"Oh, now you have a daughter. You barely even see her. You're gone by the time she wakes up and at night, you don't even come home."

"Where are you going?"

"Yasmine said that I could stay with her."

"What? Are you fucking her? I've noticed ya'll been spending a lot of time together. I don't want my daughter around that mess!"

"Omar, please. Just because I'm living with another woman doesn't mean that I'm sleeping with her. Don't try to cast your demons onto me."

"Yea, whatever. You guys are probably over there licking each other like crazy." Shanice gave him a look of disgust. "You know that I'm telling the truth."

Feeling guilty, Shanice grabbed her bags and left the room.

"Good-bye, Omar."

"I'll have the divorce papers sent to your dike girlfriend's house!"

All he heard was the door slam. He didn't give a damn. Let her go, it was for the best. Even though she still had his heart if Shanice wanted to go, let her.

He still loved her. That would never change. He knew their marriage was in shambles. He held faith that they would return to each other. Where they gone wrong?

Chapter 17

"What is she thinking? Why doesn't Carrie realize that Sami slept with Austin?" Dawn watched as Mahogany screamed at her television. "Dawn, look, look, Sami told Austin that the baby is his! Oh, snaps!" The doorbell rang. "Dawn, can you get that?" asked Mahogany. Dawn dragged herself away from the television and opened the door.

"Mahogany, I think you need to come here."

"Why? Tell whoever it is to come in."

"Alright," responded Dawn. If Mahogany had turned her head, just a little, she would have been in a state of shock. Mrs. Fox stood in the doorway looking like the imperial queen. The only ting that was missing was her crown. She did not wait for Dawn to invite her in. She swept into the apartment as if she owned it.

"Dawn, look at how stupid Carrie is, are you watching this?" Mrs. Fox had not seen her daughter in years. She looked so different. Where had her baby gone? Mahogany turned towards the doorway expecting to see Dawn, instead she saw her mother.

"Mama!" Mahogany jumped off the couch. Mrs. Fox stared her daughter down. The last time they spoke was two weeks ago, when Mahogany called her mom for some extra cash.

"And I'm happy to see you, too. Girl, come here and give your mama a hug!" Never the affectionate type, Mahogany moseyed over to her mother's open arms, obligingly giving her a hug. Looking around the apartment her mother noted, "So this is what you call home? Why is it so dirty Mahogany? I know I taught you better than this?" She waited for Mahogany's excuse. It wasn't long in coming.

"I've been busy with work and stuff." Mahogany hurriedly picked up her shoes off the floor and prayed that her mom did not go into the bathroom.

"Oh, I've just seen how busy you've been." She referred to Mahogany sitting on the couch watching Soap Operas.

"What are you doing here?" asked Mahogany.

"I thought I would surprise my beloved daughter. I have missed you. Have you missed your mother?"

"Yes, of course."

"I could tell by all the phone calls I receive, you only call when you need something. Your dad told me that he sent you fifty dollars."

"You make it sound like I never call you except for when I need something."

"You call once in a blue moon Mahogany don't stand here lying to me."

Changing the subject, Mahogany asked, "You remember Dawn, right?"

"Why, yes, I do. Hello, baby, how are you doing?"

"I'm doing fine, thank you, Mrs. Fox."

"I'm glad to hear it, now tell me what you and my daughter have been up to?"

"Working really, I work at a detective agency."

"Is that dangerous?"

"No, not really, I mainly do secretarial work."

"Well, that's interesting. I bet you get some fringe benefits working in a place like that."

Dawn nervously looked away, "That's true, I guess." Dawn got up and took her coat, "I bet you guys have a lot of catching up to do. I'm going to run to the store for a bit." Ignoring Mahogany panicked look, Dawn left.

"So tell me Mahogany, how is Shanice doing?"

"She's doing fine."

No way in the world was she going to tell her mother about Shanice's current escapade. She listened as her mother ramble off about the gossip in Idaho. It was a world that seemed so far away right now. Mahogany listened to her mother, she thought she would get a reprieve when Shanice called, but the minute Shanice heard Mrs. Fox voice, she quickly requested that Mahogany tell her mother "hello" for her and hung up the telephone. Mrs. Fox later made herself a pallet on the couch, leaving Mahogany to pray that Damien did not stop by. It was around 2:00am when Mahogany heard the door rattle.

Getting out of bed, Mahogany quietly opened the door to a drunken Dawn.

"What are you doing drunk? You know my mom is here!" whispered Mahogany. Dawn face was bright red from alcohol.

"Sorry, I forgot." Mahogany went outside of her apartment so they would not wake up her mother.

"Why are you drunk? Last thing you told me was that you were going to the store, does "store" mean "bar" to you?"

"No, but I had to go there. Your mom said something that really bothered me."

"Like what?" Her mom was low-key tonight compared to the damage she was capable of doing.

"The stuff she said about working at the detective agency, she was right."

What the hell was she talking about?

"Right about what Dawn?"

"The fringe benefits." Mahogany still was confused. "I work there so I could find my son. I miss him. I wonder what he looks like, what he's doing. I want my son. I should have never listened to Shane or my family. Where is my son? Where is my son at?"

Mahogany did not know what to say. She had not mentioned Dawn's pregnancy since high school. She knew then how much it hurt. She couldn't imagine what she was going through now. It was not as if she could relate to Dawn's agony. When Dawn called Mahogany that fateful day in high school, she offered no advice. The idea of being pregnant in high school was not something she could fathom. Mahogany only offered Dawn the decency of being non-judgmental. Watching her now, Dawn hardly believed that that was enough.

"I don't know, Dawn. I don't know." Mahogany hugged her friend who appeared to be in so much pain. "Come on inside, you need to rest."

They went inside and Mahogany tucked Dawn in her bed. Looking at the misery in her friend, Mahogany made up her mind to never do anything that went against what she believed in.

* * *

Shanice finally gathered her nerves and visited Mrs. Fox, who was more than thrilled to see her. She greeted her with open arms.

"Girl, what have you been up to? You're looking more and more like your mother. Turn around girl, let me see you." Shanice obliged, even going so far as to do a courtesy. She knew all too well the respect demanded of 'Her Royal Highness.'

"Mahogany told me that you got married and girl, I'm so proud of you. You kept your tail down and waited for marriage. Good for you." Mrs. Fox looked pointedly at Mahogany.

"Yes, I got married and had a baby. Guess now all I need is the white picket fence."

"Girl, marriage isn't all that easy. You have to put your heart and soul into it. You can't get married then decide you don't like it. Then go around sleeping with someone else when times get rough. You have to make a commitment."

"You are so right," agreed Shanice.

The women made small chat for a little bit. Shanice had to hurry back before Yasmine started to wonder what was taking her so long. She promised Mrs. Fox that she would see her again before she left. While discussing what to eat for dinner the telephone rang. Mrs. Fox answered the telephone.

"Fox residence."

"May I speak with Mahogany?"

"Who's speaking, honey?"

"Ruby from the Jazz Theater Company."

"Mahogany, it's for you."

Mahogany took the phone from her mother, "Yes, this is Mahogany." She hoped it wasn't Damien. Unfortunately, her mother knew that he existed. Her mom called when she and Damien were living together, after her mother chewed Damien's ass out, he handed the telephone to Mahogany. He left her to explain their "current" live in situation to her mother. Mahogany should have known right then that he wasn't a man.

"I did! That's great! I'll be there, thank you. Thank you."

"What was that about?" Her mother inquired.

"Guess what? I got the part!"

"What part?" quizzed Mrs. Fox.

"The part in *Ghost*, remember that movie when Whoopi Goldberg was a psychic? It had Patrick Swayze and Demi Moore in it."

Her mother could have cared less. "What about it?"

"I got the part!" Mrs. Fox was less than thrilled. Deep down she wanted so much more for Mahogany. She was disappointed in the fact that Mahogany hadn't finished school.

"Congratulations," she said dryly.

"I've got to call Shanice, she should be home by now." Mahogany quickly dialed Yasmine's telephone number.

"Hello? May I speak with Shanice?"
"Who is this?"
"Mahogany."
"Mahogany? What do you want?"
"I want to speak with Shanice."
"Why? Is there an emergency or something?"
"No, I just want to speak with her."
"Hold-on."
She heard muffled voices from the telephone.
"Hello?"
"What's up with Yasmine? Why is she so bitchy?"
"I don't know girl. We're not going to worry about that, what's up?"
"Shanice! I got the part. I'm about to be Ms. Oda May Brown. We're on our way to the big time!"
"I knew you could do it!" They spoke for several minutes. Mahogany rushed off the telephone, she had tons of things to do.

* * *

Shanice patiently watched Yasmine slam pots and pans in the kitchen.

"Do you mind telling me what your problem is?"

Yasmine shrugged, "I don't understand why she must call here every time something happens in her life. Doesn't she have friends besides you?"

"I'm quite sure she does, but Mahogany and I have been friends since we were kids."

"Ummm, yea right."

Yasmine's amused Shanice with her jealously. She kissed Yasmine on the lips.

"I'm with you, that's all you need to know. Don't be mad." They kissed passionately, proud of the fact that they were finally together.

* * *

Mahogany had survived. Her mother had stayed a whole week and Mahogany still had her sanity. She accompanied her mother to the airport.

"Oh, momma, I forgot to tell you that Jake Myers is here in Raleigh. You remember, the one with the crazy mom?"

"Mahogany, did you know that his mother died a couple of years ago." Mahogany was shocked. "Really, I wonder why he's never mentioned it to me. Wow, what happened?"

"I don't remember the details, but I think she had a heart attack or something."

"How sad."

Mahogany waited in the terminal until her mother boarded the plane. Although her mom had over stayed her welcome, she would miss her. She loved and appreciated her mother for all her faults.

Chapter 18

He was close. Very close.

The big date was near. Each day that she breathed was because he let her. He knew where she was and where she slept. She could not get away from him. Not this time. He remembered the feel of her flesh in his fingers.

Warm and hot. In a matter of days her warm blood would be flowing.

They could have had so much.

Why did the bitch have to ruin it?

There was no turning back now, the plans were in motion. And he would follow through with them. He needed redemption. He could not stop even if he wanted to.

He would be redeemed.

Chapter 19

Opening night of the play had arrived. After weeks of rehearsal Mahogany was ready. All her friends had arrived, showing their support. Peeking at the audience from backstage, Mahogany could not believe she was living her long awaited dream. She wished her mother were there. The director ordered everyone to their places. The curtain rose, the auditorium became silent, Mahogany mentally prepared herself. She loved acting and being on stage. It was in her blood.

* * *

During the play, he looked at her. He hated her even more as she pranced around the stage. Tonight was the night. Mahogany Fox's last day on earth.

* * *

Dawn watched Mahogany on stage. Her friend had waited a long time for this moment. It a strange way, Dawn watching Mahogany live out her dream on stage, gave her a unique comfort in that, as long as she did not give up hope, she would find her son. Mahogany had succeeded in something even her own mother didn't believe she could do. She still could not believe that she was sitting in the audience watching her friend. She also watched Yasmine and Shanice. Dawn noticed that they were awfully close just to be *friends*, not to mention, there was way too much touching and whispering between them. The loud applause drew her away from her thoughts. The show had ended. Dawn went backstage to wait on Mahogany.

"Hey, Dawn, give me about fifteen minutes to get this make-up off."

"Alright, I'll wait outside. It's so hot in here."

Dawn walked outside, she was positive that she saw Yasmine and Shanice holding hands, but when she looked a second time, they weren't.

Weird, weird.

Mahogany was obviously taking her sweet time. Dawn started to go into the theater for her when she saw Mahogany take the side entrance out.

Mahogany sang to herself. The play had gone off without a hitch. She was still on top of the world when she got grabbed from behind. A hand covered her mouth, stifling her scream. He managed to drag her as she kicked and fought. Her assailant seemingly prepared, used his strength to control her.

"Mahogany!" Her attacker quickly shoved her to the ground and took off running. "Mahogany, my God are you OK?" Damien cradled her body close to his.

"Damien, did you see who did this?"

He rubbed his fingers through her hair, "No, honey, he was wearing a mask."

"Who would want to do this?"

"I don't know, baby, but we're calling the police." Mahogany saw Dawn running towards them.

"What happened," she asked.

"Someone attacked Mahogany." Dawn's face became ashen. "Are you alright, Mahogany?"

"I'm fine, thank God Damien showed up when he did. That guy was trying to take me somewhere."

"Come on, we need to report this to the police," Damien said.

After filing a report, the officers advised Mahogany to be careful and to report anything out of the ordinary. Damien made it clear to Mahogany that he was moving back in. Someone had an agenda against her and it was his job to protect her.

Mahogany did not know why, but she was glad to have Damien in her apartment again. It was 4:30am when they got back from the police station. Damien ran Mahogany some bath water then washed her body for her. He could tell that deep down, she was frightened. As he helped her out of the bathtub, Mahogany decided to tell him how she felt.

"I'm glad that you are here with me."

He wrapped the towel around her and held her close. Mahogany knew in her mind that one of Damien's many girlfriends was wondering where he was. It did not bother her though. She wasn't jockin' him like she used to be, she was glad that he was with her at that very moment.

"Let's go lay down, baby."

Tonight he found out how much he really needed her in his life. She had always been there for him. Lying down, he held her tight. He never wanted to let her go. He slowly began to kiss the nape of her neck. Mahogany did not resist. She could tell by the way he was kissing her. H wanted to love her and make love to her body. She wanted him to. Damien made sweet love to Mahogany. They probably had had sex hundreds of times, but tonight he was making love to her, Mahogany Fox, for no other reason than he truly loved her. He made her body reach peaks she never had. She loved the way he made her feel, he was like a drug guaranteed to please but dangerous to your health. She fell asleep with him holding her and when she awoke he was gone.

* * *

Lt. Peck stood in the doorway of the office watching Dawn rush in late.

"I'll help you," he offered.

"Help with what?"

"Looking for your child, I know that's what you're doing here." Dawn did not need this shit. She had not gotten any sleep. Mahogany and Damien had made all kinds of noises last night. She did not feel like arguing.

"Thanks, what gave me away?"

"Well, all of those returned calls from adoption agencies in Idaho, those tend to stick out, you know."

"Yea, I guess they would." She rubbed her eyes.

"Why are you so tired?"

"My friend, Mahogany got attacked last night. We went to the opening of her play and some guy attacked her as she was leaving."

"You're kidding," he rubbed his big belly. "These days you can't be too careful."

"That's true, she's so afraid of being alone now, if I was her I'd probably feel the same way. Just knowing that there is a person out in the world who wants to do you harm is scary enough." She prayed that Shane was not involved.

"Maybe we can find out who is it."

"I doubt it. I hope whoever it was is long gone by now. I hope that it was one of those random acts of violence and that no one has a vendetta against her."

Lt. Peck rubbed his chin, "We'll see."

Chapter 20

Sex was not everything. A hard lesson to learn, but it's true. Shanice cared for Yasmine, but there was something about her that bothered Shanice. For example, the fact she used to be or still is promiscuous rubbed Shanice the wrong way. Last night when they were talking about sex, Yasmine revealed how much she enjoyed riding men, which wasn't a problem. It was something that Shanice rather enjoyed too. However, when Yasmine clarified, "Yea, I like riding it in the ass." Shanice thought she was going to throw up. It was a compilation of things that bothered Shanice. Yasmine friends would come over at all times of the night without calling. It was fine with Yasmine, but Shanice hated it. She hated the fact that she had her daughter in such an environment. If Omar had any idea, he would take Shante away without thinking twice. Shanice continued to lie about how her and Yasmine were just "friends." The only reason he believed her was because he loved her. She wasn't ready to tell him everything yet. She doubted if she ever would.

*   *   *

After work Mahogany waited for Damien in the parking lot. Boy did she get a reality check. She saw Damien kissing one of his many flavors and it caused a rainbow of emotions to erupt within her. Her brain knew Damien was not hers, but her heart had a problem understanding that. Especially after last night. Turning away before he spotted her, Mahogany walked to her car.

"Hey, Mahogany?"

"Oh, Hi Jake. I didn't see you."

"I know. I saw you checking out your ex, I didn't want to interrupt you. Is everything cool?"

"It's going to be if I can help it. He's not obligated to me, he can see whoever he wants." Jake could tell that she was hurt and upset. "It just takes some time getting used to it when it's right in front of your face, you know."

"You feel like going out tonight? Maybe I could come over to your place."

Mahogany agreed, "That would be nice."

"Let me get my stuff, and then we could leave. Wait for me." After Jake left, Damien came over to speak with her.

"How is everything?"

"Just fine," replied Mahogany. He didn't promise her anything last night did he? She missed Damien, but not the drama.

"Good, good. Do you want me to come over tonight?"

"No. Jake is keeping me company, thanks anyway." He stood there looking at her like he wanted to tell her something. The moment passed as quickly as it started.

"Oh. As long as you're okay, you know that I worry about you." Mahogany stared at his back as he walked off.

Shortly after Jake returned, they left. She was happy that he was coming over. Dawn had called excited about some lead on her son, so she wouldn't be home until late. She did not want to be left alone.

Chapter 21

"Well, looky here," Lt. Peck typed furiously at his computer. "Eureka! Dawn, I'm going to check this out."

"What out?" she asked. What was he up to now?

"Remember that list of friends I had you make of your friend Mahogany?"

"Yea. Did anything turn up?"

"Maybe. Follow me. "Hurry up, hurry."

*　　　　　*　　　　　*

Mahogany quickly opened her apartment door. Jake was dangerously close to dropping the grocery bag. Placing the bags on the floor Jake observed her apartment.

"You have a nice place here, do you like it?"

"What do you mean, 'do you like it?' It's my home, of course, I like it."

"I wasn't criticizing it. Just making sure you're content."

"Well, I am. Why don't you start cooking dinner?"

They had decided on spaghetti with meatballs. His specialty he claimed. They chatted about old times as he prepared the food. "So who taught you how to cook this specialty?"

"My mom. Remember how my mom hated every time you said a simple "hello" to me?"

"Really Jake, She had a problem with that?"

"Just a little one."

"I'm sorry to hear about your mother."

"What about her?"

"Well, my mother told me that she passed away a couple of years ago. I'm sorry to hear about it, the way you talk about her I would think that you speak to her everyday."

"I like to think that I do."

"That's nice," agreed Mahogany.

He laughed nervously, "I almost got you back, you know."

"For what?" Mahogany was confused. Did he play a practical joke on her and she did not know about it?

"My mom."

"How did you almost get me?"

"Remember in high school, I think you walking toward the Youth Center? And you were attacked, well, almost raped." He was sixteen years old when the lust over took his heart. He could not contain it. He had bided his time, waiting for the right time to get her. He thought about that night. He dressed carefully, wearing gloves and a mask. He had followed her a couple of times before replaying how he would fulfill himself within her body. He regretted it every day that he lost his chance because of her stupid friend. That day had finally been given to him again. This time it will not be ruined.

"How did you know that?" demanded Mahogany.

Jake continued, "You were so lucky that your dear friend Shanice rescued you, huh?"

"Who told you that?" yelled Mahogany.

"No one, sweetie. I was there."

"You were there? How were you...?" Mahogany covered her mouth as Jake took a knife from his jacket drawer. He watched her eyes dart nervously around.

"Yes, it was I. Uh-uh, I wouldn't think about running if I were you. Once I catch you, it could get nasty."

"Jake?" She was terrified. Something was terribly wrong with him. Maybe she could reason with him. His eyes had changed, he wasn't even Jake anymore. Panic flooded her body.

"Why are you doing this?"

"My mother. I loved my mother. She hated me for wanting you. A black woman. A black sin. Dark and void. I wanted to sin. My mother was just trying to protect me from sin. Don't you understand? Every night she would take a knife and make me bleed for wanting you." He lifted her shirt and Mahogany felt the bile rise in her throat. Jake's chest was covered with scars, at least hundreds of them. It was a horrible sight. It looked as if he had been repeatedly stabbed.

"Don't be afraid, she never actually stabbed deep enough to do any damage. She always threatened to cut my heart out." He rubbed each grotesque scar. "She never did though. She wanted to make sure that I knew you were to blame." He moved closer, touching the blade to her throat.

"I'm sorry for what I'm about to do."

* * *

"I can't believe we're doing this."

"Believe it, honey."

Dawn stood as a look out as Lt. Peck picked the lock to Jake's apartment.

"Tell me again why were here."

"Your friend Jake has a record. It seems he was under suspicion for the murder of his mother. She had a heart attack, but the cops thought he had something to do with it."

"That's it?"

"That's it."

The lock surrendered to Lt. Peck experienced hands. Once inside neither could find their voice. Pictures of Mahogany covered every corner of the walls. There were pictures that seemed to cover every aspect of her life dating back from high school to the present.

They had to find Mahogany quick.

*   *   *

Mahogany lost count of the number of times Jake stabbed her. She was bleeding heavily and she was losing consciousness.

"Jake, please, let me go. The police are going to know that you did this to me. I told Damien that you were coming over."

"That's nice, I'll just tell them that when I came over, I found you dead. Seeing how you're about to die."

"Please let me go."

Jake ignored her annoying pleads. He seemed fascinated with the blood flowing from Mahogany's body. The redemption was near. He hated her for making him hurt his mother. He could not help it that he wanted her body, her flesh, and the sin. Before passing out, Mahogany saw Jake pick up the knife one last final time.

*   *   *

Dawn did not know what to think as Lt. Peck sped to Mahogany's apartment.

"That guy is sick. I've seen a lot of strange things in my day, but…"

"Will you shut up and drive faster," ordered Dawn. "Make a left here, this is it"

Dawn jumped out of the car before it came to a complete stop. Lt. Peck was hot on her heels. Using her key, Dawn crept into the apartment. She did not see anyone. The only thing she saw was a large pool of blood.

"Mahogany!"

She was about to go into Mahogany's bedroom when a burning sensation ran down her back. Pain shot down her body. Dawn did not have chance to identify the source of her pain, a hail of gunfire broke out, knocking her to the ground.

Epilogue

She had been released from the hospital two weeks ago.

Jake was dead.

If Dawn had arrived five minutes later, Mahogany would be in the same company. Lt. Peck shot Jake before he could complete his reign of terror. Mahogany still was in shock from Jake's attack.

How could he hate her so much?

The hospital nurse informed her that she was pregnant. Mahogany remembered opening night of play. Damien had her heart and soul that night. Twenty-three years old and pregnant. She told Damien the news; he claimed that he would be there for her and their child.

Time would tell.

Shanice moved out of Yasmine's house, citing that she wanted to give Omar another chance. She finally admitted to Mahogany that she had gotten too caught up with Yasmine. She missed her husband and she was more than willing to try harder on their marriage. She learned a hard lesson by allowing lust to lead your life.

Dawn was more determined than ever to find her son, she had a lead in California. Mahogany promised that she would help Dawn with anything that she needed.

Mahogany enjoyed walking the path of the unknown. Although, she was carrying his child, Mahogany did not need Damien in her life. She would make it just fine on her own.

"Mahogany?"

"Yes, Shanice."

"What are you thinking about?"

They were at Shanice's house eating dinner. Mahogany had been awfully quiet since her ordeal. Shanice was worried.

"God."

"What about him?"

"Just understanding that if I want my life to change, I need, no have to put more faith in Him than I have been."

"I know, so do I."

Neither one knew what the future held for them. After all they had experienced. They were ready for anything.

Love. Mahogany had agreed that she was deeply in lust with Damien. Shanice admitted that she was deeply attracted to Yasmine. Their decisions had lasting effects, leaving a mark on their life forever. Yesterday was gone, tomorrow was a day both held preciously. Future tomorrows were unique. Shanice would use each day rebuilding her marriage. Mahogany would use each day looking forward to the birth of her child. Starting then, that moment, life began anew for them.

About the Author

Nevada York began writing after high school. *Caught Up* is her first novel. Ms. York lives in North Carolina with her daughter, and is currently working on a new novel. Find out more about Nevada on her website: *http://nevadayork.tripod.com/nevadayork*

0-595-18737-4

Printed in the United States
35725LVS00006B/357